The Curious Haun
An Order

By
Conrad Jones

RED DRAGON BOOKS

copyright@conradjones2023

THIS BOOK IS AN ACCURATE account of what happened at 44 Brick Street. Part of the story is written as I understand it happened, because I wasn't there, and the rest is my exact recollection of events. This is not cozy crime fiction or a pleasant read. If you scare easily, go no further into this dark world...

Conrad

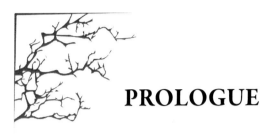

PROLOGUE

L iverpool 2021

CAROL HARRIS STARED out of the rain-spattered window of Quick Move UK estate agents and sighed. She stretched her arms above her head and checked the clock for the umpteenth time that morning. The huge station clock on the wall looked very fashionable and in keeping with the minimalist furnishings, but it made it impossible to avoid how painfully slowly the time passed. Since Covid arrived, seconds were minutes, minutes became hours and a full day shift felt like a week. The raindrops trickled down the glass, gathering momentum along the way. A steady stream of water poured over the sill, splashing onto the already saturated pavement. Deep puddles formed between the uneven slabs. People wearing facemasks sidestepped each other, frightened to be near other humans. They dodged the larger puddles as they ran for cover from the deluge, their umbrellas tilted against the driving rain, hats pulled down and collars pulled up, masks on.

Carol watched the passers-by doing just that, passing by. The weather and Covid-19 seemed to be conspiring against her to stop people from looking at the properties in her window. Everything was moving online but if they didn't look in the window, then they didn't buy. She had been in the housing business for nearly twenty years, but she'd never known the property market so depressed. There'd been lean times, admittedly, but this virus-driven recession was the worst she could ever remember. If it wasn't for the internet, she would be out of business.

The high street was dying a death before the virus arrived, now it was terminal. Even when it wasn't raining, no one enquired about the properties that they had for sale. She could count the number of house hunters who had stepped through the door in the last week on two hands, three at best. She asked herself constantly why no one was interested in looking at the 'for sale' ads display in the windows. They couldn't catch the virus through the glass.

The phone rang and she looked at it as if she had never seen it before. There had been an increase in enquiries online and on the phone, but they were mostly curious and spurious. Unicorn hunters, she called them. They were the people who would ask every question about the property that they could think of until she told them something they didn't like. Then they would grimace and shake their heads and sound disappointed.

'Shame, we really liked it until you told us that...'

'What you're really looking for is a property with a unicorn in the back garden...' she would think.

Or there were the people who just wanted to know how much their neighbour's house had sold for. These days she would have been grateful for even a few of those customers. Six months ago, the high street business had tapered to two sales per month but now even that seemed busy. Nobody was interested in buying or selling and no one could view anything in person. Virtual viewings were happening, but they weren't the same. The purchase rate was much lower, below half. If things carried on as they were, she would have to seriously consider cutting the number of staff and going to an online business only. She only had two staff and they were driving her insane. They were constantly phoning in sick, trying to be allowed to work from home. Furlough had nearly broken her as the government was so slow in releasing money to businesses.

Barry Bishop had been with her the longest; the smart-arse, back-stabbing, double-crossing little shit that he was. Through furlough, he had sold properties from under her, she knew that he had but she couldn't prove it. He was a good salesman; there was no denying that, when there was anyone to sell to, that was. Carol would far rather sack him and keep Carrie Drake in the job. She had watched her at work many times. When she was dealing with their male customers, there wasn't a seller in the city who could match her conversion rate. If the customer had a cock, she could sell them a house. Carrie bragged that it was nothing to do with her long dark hair, flirty eyes and her fantastic long legs. Of course, she always did a twirl and wiggled her sexy arse when she said it, but then that was part of her joke. Carrie used her sexuality to sell and that was fine with Carol.

Carol wasn't from the island of Lesbos, and she didn't even want to go there on a day trip, but she could appreciate how sexy Carrie was. Lucky bitch. She had pretty much everything a girl could want. She swore blind that her tits were real, but the way they defied gravity? Carol wasn't convinced. Anyway, the long and short of it was that if push came to shove, then Barry Bishop would be a footnote in estate agent history.

Carol dragged her eyes from the clock and reached for her mobile again. No calls and no messages. She was setting a bad example to her staff. Using their mobiles during work hours was discouraged but not forbidden. She had thought about banning them, but it was 2021, how could she? She owned the business and, yet the boredom was killing her. They had already cold-called all their internet customers and there were only so many times that they could try to sell a bigger house to their existing customers.

'We have a new property in our portfolio. Are you looking to upgrade your home yet?'

'No. Do you know there's a pandemic going on?'

She looked around the office. Barry was on the phone, gabbling away as usual, giving the poor recipient the 'benefit' of his sales spiel by describing the advantages of moving to a bungalow after reaching the age of sixty, in anticipation of the onset of arthritis or other debilitating illnesses. He had his feet on the desk, his patent brogues gleaming and his superhero socks on show to the world. Today they were Iron Man.

Knobhead.

He was leaning back in his chair as if he owned the place. Carol had told him a million times not to do that just in case a customer walked in to browse. Barry had laughed and replied that it was very unlikely that that would happen. Carol felt like going over to him and flinging his legs in the air so that he toppled backwards onto the floor, but the fear of a tribunal stopped her from doing so.

The clinking of cups in the small kitchen area to the rear told her that Carrie was busy making coffee, and the aroma was making her salivate. She always looked forward to their mid-morning coffee and biscuits, one, because she was peckish by then and loved coffee and two, because it signalled the first part of the morning shift was complete. Recently, Barry had started to pop round to Starbucks, saying that the coffee 'dust' that Carol bought them was undrinkable. Ungrateful little shit.

She could buy a jar of coffee dust, as he called it, for what he paid for a large latte. If he could afford to buy their coffee, then she was paying him too much, or he was moonlighting which would explain a lot. She had a hunch that he was directing would-be sellers to another estate agent and then taking a backhander from them. It was a good plan. He got his wages from Carol and kickbacks with absolutely no selling involved. The conniving little shit. Covid was great news for conmen. There were so many opportunities, especially when they worked from home.

Carol felt anger growing in her guts as she glanced back at the window. Carrie put her coffee down in front of her and smiled behind her mask.

'Is it okay to take my mask off while I drink this?' Carrie asked, taking off her mask.

'Of course.' Carol took off her mask and sipped her coffee. 'Wearing these is ridiculous. I don't want a fine, so needs must.'

'My fella says wearing a mask is like pissing at the other end of the swimming pool,' Carrie said.

'I don't get it,' Carol said, frowning.

'Well,' Carrie said, 'Neither do I, to be honest. He's not the brightest bulb on the tree.'

'Why do you see him then?'

'Huge knob,' Carrie said, smiling.

Carol smiled back and then noticed that there was movement in the window. At last, somebody was looking in the window at the ads and browsing the photographs. It was sad that she felt such a twinge of joy at the sight of a window-shopper but that was how business had taken her. Her joy was tempered by the fact that she noticed Carrie had given Barry two plain biscuits with his coffee. That signalled that all the chocolate digestives had been eaten and she wondered who had eaten the last one without saying anything again. That would be Barry Bishop, no doubt. Little shit. He was making her spend a fortune on biscuits, the greedy bastard. And what had she got to show for it?

His last sale on her behalf had been nearly three months ago. The maths just didn't add up. It just couldn't go on. It would have to be plain biscuits on a permanent basis at this rate. Either that or she would need to make Barry redundant. Carol really didn't want any confrontation, but it was on the cards. She didn't trust him anyhow, so why hadn't she done it sooner?

She debated the situation in her mind while she studied the young man who was standing in the pouring rain, crouched under a broken umbrella, the spokes threatening people as they squeezed past him on the narrow pavement. The wind must have turned his umbrella inside out. Pound-shop rubbish just didn't last but then who expected it to If he was buying crappy umbrellas, could he be a possible buyer? He looked very young but then most first-time buyers looked way too young nowadays. She was feeling her age lately. Maybe he was young and rich. Perhaps his parents were buying him his first flat. She was still toying with the possibilities when the doorbell buzzed, and her first potential customer for weeks stood dripping on the laminate floor before her.

'Do I need to wear a mask?' he asked. 'I'm not coming in if I have to wear a mask.'

'We will maintain social distancing and that will suffice.' She smiled at him sympathetically. 'You look like you need a hot drink.' she stepped towards him and pointed at the tattered umbrella. 'Can you put that over there please.'

He held it over the entry mat to stop it from forming a puddle in the office.

'Shall I put it against the wall?'

'Yes. Can I get you a tea or a coffee?'

'You read my mind,' Jerry Bracknall said shaking the rain from his shoes. 'I'll have a tea, please, white with two sugars.'

'Carrie, could you make –' She paused and turned to the damp young man. 'Sorry, what was your name?'

'Jerry.'

'Jerry,' she smiled. 'Could you make Jerry a tea, please, white with two sugars.'

'Okay,' Carrie answered, heading to the kitchen.

'Now, what is it that you're looking for?' Carol asked. It had been a while, but you never lose your touch, she thought. 'Flat, house or bungalow?'

'Flat, I think,' he said shrugging his shoulders. 'At least that is what I think I want.'

'Okay,' Carol guided him to the left-hand wall where all the flats were displayed. 'Here are all our flats.' She waved her hands as she spoke. 'The lower-priced properties are to the left and our more expensive flats are on the right.' Her heart sank as he instinctively stepped to the left, ignoring the right. He wasn't a young entrepreneur looking for a penthouse. Her beaming smile narrowed somewhat.

'Tea for Jerry?' Carrie appeared next to them. 'I'm wearing gloves, so you can touch the cup.'

'Thanks,' Jerry said smiling.

'You're more than welcome, you poor thing,' she said. 'You're soaked though.' She had analysed the young man from head to toe with a glance. The sparkle in her eyes told Carol that she was interested in more than just a sale, which was good, as she could leave her to it. 'Would you like me to take Jerry through our portfolio?' she asked. Carol winked and stepped back. 'Have you seen anything you fancy?' she teased. 'I'm Carrie, by the way.'

'Hello Carrie.'

Jerry sipped his tea and scanned the price boards. He could see at once that the price of the flats on sale were way beyond his budget, but he noticed that the pretty estate agent was eyeing him hopefully. She had ten years on him, but she was attractive alright. He felt a little awkward as he browsed. Being the only customer in the shop meant that three sets of eyes were focused on him. It was as if they were waiting for him to take out his wallet right there and then. Business didn't look too good for them. Jerry grinned to himself, as it might be a good thing for him. Estate agents had had a good run for their money, he reflected smugly, so it was about time they felt the pinch like everybody else. In his opinion, estate agents were only one notch up from bankers, traffic wardens and dog shit. Still, it was warm and dry, and the tea was hot, so was Carrie. He thought he might as well go on with the charade and see if there was anything remotely within his budget. If business was slow, asking prices could be slashed.

Jerry watched with amusement as Carrie hovered around him but kept the two meters distance required. He wondered if she would be such a flirt if he wasn't a potential buyer.

'I'm just looking for a rough idea of prices at the moment.' He slurped his tea. 'Are the properties advertised here typical of what's available?' He laughed sourly. 'Because I really can't afford anything here.'

Carol listened to them and eyed the young man closely. He was a clean-cut six-footer with dark, wavy hair, the type to appeal to women of all ages, like someone from a Coke advert. He was probably looking for a flashy pad, to take the current shag to impress the knickers off her but he couldn't do it on the budget of a minimum wage earner. Well, good luck to him, she thought, but he wouldn't get what he wanted from her unless he had the cash.

The going rate was the going rate and that couldn't be changed no matter how good looking the client. She couldn't find him a studio flat overlooking the river for the price of a repossessed shed in Chernobyl. What could she do about it? Carrie was great at selling but she wasn't a magician. If he didn't have the money, then they were wasting their time.

'I'm afraid that the flats we have are all around the same sort of starting price, depending on location, number of bedrooms, decorative condition,' Carol told him from her desk. 'If the prices quoted are too high for you, then I'm sorry, but I don't think we can help you.'

'Okay, not to worry.' Jerry handed Carrie his empty cup, shrugged and turned to leave.

Barry spoke up. 'What about that house in Brick Street, Carol?' A crooked smile crossed his lips and there was a sinister look in his eyes. 'Have you shown the young gentleman that?'

'No,' Carol stuttered. She blushed and looked embarrassed. 'It is at the cheaper end of the market, Jerry but it is a house, not a flat.' She rummaged for some paperwork. 'Would you look at a terraced house?'

'I would look at a garage at the moment,' he joked. 'I need a bit of privacy,' he added, looking at Carrie. She blushed and returned his smile. 'I play the drums you see.'

'Oh,' Carrie said as she stopped smiling. She looked disappointed.

'I'm joking,' Jerry laughed.

'Oh, cheeky!'

'Yes, I need my own place because my girlfriend screams like a banshee!'

'OMG. Too much information!' Carrie stopped laughing again and flushed red. She wasn't sure if she was embarrassed or angry now. 'I don't think we need to know that.'

'That was a joke too. I'm single.'

'Oh! I see,' she said, embarrassed now. 'More tea?' she asked, walking away to hide her blushes.

'That would be great,' Jerry called after her. 'Why is this house so cheap then?'

'It is a property that has been on the market for over ten years,' Barry chuckled. 'It hasn't been sold for the simple reason that it is in dire need of renovation.'

That's what we tell potential buyers, anyway, Barry thought, smiling at Carol.

However, there probably wasn't any foundation to the rumours surrounding the house's past. That was all just mumbo-jumbo.

'Of course, Barry is right.' She turned back to Jerry and gave him an appraising look. He seemed a down-to-earth sort of guy, hardly likely to be phased by talk of ancient burial pits, murders, ghosts and such like. Anyway, it wasn't up to Carol to inform him of the stories circulating about the house being haunted. Even if the truth was that it was the main reason it was still on the market after such a long time.

'Do you think you would be interested in an old terrace?' Carol took out a flyer from the bottom drawer of her filing cabinet. 'If you're on a seriously tight budget then this property might suit you,' she said, offering it to him. 'Compared to other properties in the same area, this little terraced house is quite a bargain. The potential is enormous.'

The young man took it from her tentatively and studied it.

'This wasn't in the window, was it? I don't remember seeing it.' He looked at her as he spoke.

Carol coughed nervously. 'No. It hasn't been a best-seller, this one. As you can see, there's an obvious reason for that.' Jerry looked at the photo of the run-down terraced house, squashed in between two much smarter-looking dwellings. Their windows and doors were double-glazed units in PVC frames whereas number 44 had the original wooden sash frames. The glass was blackened with grime, the wood cracked and warped. Four ridge tiles were missing from the roof, the slates crooked and the lead flashing was corroded by time and the elements. It certainly didn't seem very promising on the face of it. 'It needs a lot of work.'

'I think it needs more work than I could afford, to be honest.' He cocked his head to one side thoughtfully. 'Although, some of my friends are builders.'

'It wouldn't have to be done all at once unless you were looking to sell it on quickly.' Carol felt sorry for the young man, so many of his age group were in the same boat. She wondered how on earth could they ever going to get on the property ladder these days with lending so tight. 'It could be done as a live-in project.'

'I have very little capital to play with,' he said, looking at the images of the house. It didn't look like a welcoming home, in fact to say the house was uninviting, was to understate the case by a gargantuan amount. 'I think my capital would be swallowed up by a deposit on the finance. It would take that amount again and then double it to make it watertight.'

Not only was it in a very dilapidated state, but it also looked strangely foreboding. The darkness behind the windows seemed infinite. He rubbed his eyes as he stared at the pictures. It had an eerie air of abandonment about it. He shook his head and smiled thinly to himself. Looking at the photograph, he thought he had seen a shape at the bedroom window looking back at him but then that would be madness. A shiver ran down his spine and he suddenly felt a chill.

'Are you cold?' Carrie asked as she returned from the kitchen and noticed him shivering. 'Here is your tea. Drink it. It will warm you up.'

'Thanks.' He took the cup as he spoke. Carol and Carrie looked at each other as his hand trembled, spilling the tea a little. 'I'm so sorry,' he apologised. 'Someone just walked over my grave.'

'Don't worry, you're just cold and wet,' Carrie said chirpily. 'I'll get a mop, don't worry about it.'

Jerry felt weird. Something had spooked him, but he didn't know what. The house was a shambles, but it was a house of sorts and although it would need renovating from top to bottom to make it habitable, this didn't put him off. If the price was right, then he could be interested.

'Don't go near it again,' a voice whispered. He shivered again.

'What did you say?' Jerry asked Carrie.

'I didn't say anything,' she said, shaking her head.

'I warned you. Stay away from it...' the voice whispered.

'It's very run-down of course,' Jerry stammered. He felt his knees trembling. 'What's the vendor asking for it?'

Carol riffled through her file and coughed nervously again. She already knew the answer to that one, but she faked the search anyway. 'The odd thing is that there is no asking price.'

'What do you mean?' Jerry asked.

'Stay away...'

'Just that. There is no asking price.' She smiled. 'The vendors are living in Spain and just want shot of it. Any price you care to name will be considered. Within reason, of course,' she added, thinking about the commission she would receive.

'Of course.' Jerry smiled nervously. 'What's the catch?'

'Death is the catch...' the whisperer said. *'Your death..'*

'Catch?'

'Yes, what is the catch? The property is obviously in need of a renovation, but it's in a fashionable part of the city and looking at the adjacent properties, I can see great possibilities for it. So, if I offer a price well below its market value and I'm accepted, well, there must be a catch.'

'Leave now...'

'I think it's just that the owners need ready cash to continue living the lifestyle they've got in Spain.' She shrugged. 'They've bought another property out there and it's in need of renovation too, so they need to get their hands on some money quickly.'

'How long has it been on the market again?' Jerry asked. He felt hot sweat trickling down his spine, despite shivering.

'Take heed, fool. Stay away...'

'Over ten years,' Carol said, truthfully. 'But most people don't want to be bothered with refurbishment. They just want to move in as is. If there's a new fitted kitchen, modern bathroom, wooden floors throughout and magnolia on the walls, they're happy. Most people don't have much imagination.'

'Okay,' Jerry said. 'I'm interested to view it at least. It can't do any harm to have a look at the place.'

'Harm? You have no idea, idiot...'

'Exactly!' Carol said, scarcely able to conceal her excitement at getting a sniff of interest in a property she thought was unsaleable. 'But don't expect all mod cons. As you can see from the details, it's a dump.'

'Is that modern estate agent jargon?' Jerry grinned. 'I didn't think words like 'dump' were in your selling vocabulary.'

'No, well you can see from the pictures that it's neglected.' She shrugged. 'There's no point in saying the property is well maintained, because it isn't. As soon as you walk through the door, you'll realise that it needs work but you're a man with vision, I can tell.'

Smarmy bitch, Jerry thought but he smiled at Carol anyway. 'Well, I'm a man with a lot of vision and very little capital, that's for sure. So, needs must, as they say. Can we go and see it now?'

'Certainly,' Carol said, she turned to grab her jacket. She glared at Barry Bishop for mentioning the godforsaken place. 'Barry, can you get me the keys to 44, please.'

Barry disappeared into the back of the shop, returning swiftly with a set of keys. He dangled them into her hand as if they were red hot.

'Thanks,' said Carol. She tilted her head and smiled crookedly. 'On second thoughts, I think it's better if you take Jerry, please, Barry, what with the property being empty for so long. It would be much safer if a man goes.' She dropped the keys back into his outstretched hand. He grimaced and shook his head.

'What ever happened to equality?' he mumbled. He reached for his jacket and picked up a Slazenger golf umbrella. 'Let's go and get this over, young man. It's not far from here in the car. It's stopped raining, so we'll be fine getting to the car park.'

'I have my car behind the shops,' Jerry said. 'I'll meet you there.'

44 BRICK STREET

THE TWO MEN MADE THE journey in separate vehicles. There was no need to travel together and risk becoming infected. Besides, they both knew that they had nothing in common. Jerry took an instant dislike to Barry Bishop and Barry objected to the fact that Jerry was younger and far better looking. He looked down his nose at the younger man and Jerry didn't like that. He was an arrogant arsehole. Jerry drove behind him and his driving mirrored his general attitude to others in that he switched lanes and cut people up on the left, right and centre. Jerry tried to ignore the blaring horns. They parked up and walked the short distance to the terrace. Number 44 lived up to its apt description as a 'dump'.

'So, this is it,' Barry said, disinterested. He really hoped the young man would take one look and walk away. 'What do you think?'

'I thought the photo was bad enough, but the real thing is much worse.' Jerry took a few steps backwards to see the roof. 'When was that picture taken?'

'When it went on the market.' Barry shrugged as he spoke. 'Why?'

'Look at the state of the roof,' Jerry pointed with his hand. 'The photograph showed a few missing tiles but that must have been ten years ago!' There was a hole ten slates wide. The branches of a sapling were poking through the rafters. 'There is a tree growing out of the roof.'

'Birds.'

'What?'

'Birds,' Barry repeated. 'They eat seeds and then shit them out. You never know where they will germinate but my guess is that has grown from a seed which was dropped by a bird.'

'Interesting,' Jerry mumbled. What an idiot, he thought.

'Stay out, fool...'

'The roof isn't as bad as it looks.'

'Well, it can't be any worse than it looks!'

'The owners of the neighbouring properties were concerned that damp could spread to their buildings. We had a contractor come in and seal it from the inside with polythene membrane. The tiles need to be replaced, but it's dry inside.'

'That's something, I suppose.'

'Yes, well that's why I wasn't going to bother to lie to you about the place,' Barry lied. 'I'll understand if you want to leave it. I'll tell the boss it was too much work for you.'

'No. Let's go in anyway.' Jerry gritted his teeth as a white-hot pain shot through his front teeth. 'What the fuck?' he muttered, holding his mouth.

'Are you okay?' Barry asked, frowning.

'Yes. Let's do this.'

'Stay out!'

He had to go inside. The compulsion to enter it was overwhelming. There was no way that he couldn't go back. The fact that it had started to rain again didn't help either. Mind you, even if the sun had been blazing down, it would still have looked like a shithole. He felt a desolate sense of dread and a feeling of terrible loss. He couldn't understand his apprehension, nor could he understand the irresistible urge to go in. Again. Every sensible part of his brain was screaming at him to walk away, yet he felt utterly compelled to go in. 'I would like to look around.'

'Are you sure?' Barry frowned. He had the same feeling inside; grief and loss. It was a yearning for something that he couldn't explain. He didn't want to go in, but he felt adrenalin coursing through his veins. Stepping into the dereliction would be exciting. He couldn't understand the desire to look inside. 'We could not go inside and say that we did?'

Jerry glanced in his direction and walked up to the front door. He tried to see past the grimy windows but the darkness inside was impenetrable. It was like ink. Black but fluid as if it was moving. He thought he saw a face looking back at him but then it vanished. 'I would really like to see inside.' Barry looked blank and shrugged. 'I said, I want to go inside.'

'I'll open the door for you,' Barry said. 'You can have a quick look around.'

'Not a chance, mate,' Jerry said. 'I want you to go first and make sure I don't fall through a floor somewhere.'

As they approached the door, the feeling intensified. Jerry felt sadness like never before. A tear ran from his eye, and he wiped it away and looked at the moisture on his hand as if it wasn't his. Fear gripped him, flushing the grief away, then anger joined the mix. He felt rage fill him, anger so intense he could have stabbed Barry in the face with a spoon if he spoke. It subsided slowly but he was very confused by the waves of emotions that were hitting him.

Barry looked to be struggling too. His fingers were shaking as he tried to get the key in the hole. He had trouble turning the key in the rust-jammed lock, but eventually it turned. Barry shoved the door with his shoulder, and it opened an inch. There was a shuffling sound from behind the door. Paper rustling. He heaved at the door and the small mountain of junk mail and free papers toppled over. The door moved slightly with a groan and then gave a little more. After one more push they were inside.

Jerry stepped over the threshold and the temperature drop was startling. He guessed it was six degrees cooler inside if not more. His breath made a plume of vapour. He rubbed his hand together to keep the creeping cold from his fingers. The smell was the second thing that hit him like a smack in the face with a poo-bat. It was a putrid stench. Decay. Decomposition. Jerry pitched it somewhere between sour milk and rotting chicken. He fought the urge to gag. The cloying smell clung to the back of his throat. He could almost taste the decomposition in the air.

'Jesus!' Jerry said covering his mouth. 'Something has died in here.'

'No shit, Sherlock.'

'No, something has died in here,' Jerry repeated.

Barry wrinkled his nose. He had to agree. It was as if something had died in there several months ago. Nothing could describe it. Jerry took out his hanky and covered his nose. Barry did likewise. He couldn't remember the last time he had been here, but he was sure the smell hadn't been that bad then.

'Very strong, isn't it?' Barry said, his voice muffled by the hanky. 'Sorry about that. Must be rats or mice dead under the floorboards, I suppose.'

'I hope it's not only rats and mice,' Jerry said, his voice a whisper. 'I know it's not...'

'Pardon?' Barry asked.

'You know what it is. Leave now...'

'It smells like something much bigger than a rat. Like a hippo or an elephant or something else huge.'

Barry grimaced but said nothing. In his line of business, he was used to making excuses for poorly-maintained properties; after all, it was his stock-in-trade. But even he couldn't think of a single redeeming thing to say about the house. The smell was all consuming. He wasn't even sure the smell was simply dead rodents. After all, he knew more about the house than Jerry did, much more. His imagination conjured up images of dead bodies bound and gagged in the crawl space beneath his feet. He shook them away with the shake of his head.

'Why don't you tell him?' a voice whispered in his mind.

'Well, come on, you might as well have a look around now you're here. Don't say no outright, not yet anyway.'

'Look, Mr, er?'

'Bishop, Barry Bishop.'

'Look, Barry,' he said. 'My name is not Jerry. I think it's dangerous for you to go any further.'

Barry looked confused, but he shook his hand anyway. He was relieved that Jerry or whoever he was didn't want to go on.

'I'm glad you've seen enough. This place is awful. I can't see you or anyone else living here, ever. The place is crawling.'

'Yes, I can understand that. Perhaps you're right.' Jerry smiled. 'However, I've just seen something which might change your mind.' He looked behind Barry and a dreamy look came over his face. It was as if someone had turned off the lights behind his eyes. A strong breeze blew, and the rotting stench seemed to become stronger, almost overpowering. He felt movement around his feet and looked down to see cockroaches and earwigs scarpering over his shiny brogues. He instinctively kicked out, shaking the disgusting insects from his shoes. A powerful gust blew down the stairs. The front door slammed shut blocking out the light. It was almost pitch black but not quite. Barry turned around, frightened and confused, his breath became trapped in his lungs. As his eyes adjusted to the gloom, his jaw dropped open.

A naked woman stepped from the inky blackness of the cellar door, beneath the staircase. Her long black hair was loose around her shoulders, almost covering her bare breasts. Barry couldn't take his eyes from the tattooed artwork on her skin. She was covered from head to toe in script. Crazy swirls of scriptures, unrecognisable symbols and religious iconology covered every inch of skin from the neck down and the wrists up. Barry stared at her, unable to comprehend the image before him. She stepped forward and smiled. Her face was angelic, yet her eyes were like pools of tar set in an alabaster face. Tiny orbs of light seemed to flash across them.

'Come to me and meet Galia,' she rasped. She smiled but it wasn't a welcoming smile. Her full lips were deep red, almost black, and her teeth were crooked and stained with blood. She held a wicked blade in her right hand. It was curved like a scythe. The razor-sharp steel glinted as she moved. His legs trembled, and his heart pounded in his chest. He instinctively stepped back away from her. She reached for him with both arms. He turned quickly. His feet stumbled on the mouldy junk mail, and he bolted for the front door. He might have made it too, but Jerry stuck out his leg and sent him headlong into the wall.

'Sorry, Barry,' Jerry whispered. 'I had to feed her.'

Barry felt his head thump against the wall and his front teeth cracked against the skirting board. The taste of blood mingled with dank musty filth. His mouth filled with blood and saliva. He tried to spit it out but the weight of someone jumping on him forced the air from his chest. Bent double at an awkward angle, the force caused excruciating pain in his lower back. He twisted to escape the crushing weight. In the darkness he could just make out her features. Her pretty face was twisted into a mask of pure hate; teeth bared, snapping together like a rabid dog. Saliva drooled from the corners of her lips, and he could smell decay on her fetid breath. The blade glinted above him. He felt her nails clawing at his face, scratching at his eyes. He gave one last determined effort to shove the writhing woman from him and escape her frenzied attack, but she was too powerful. She had the strength of the possessed. Barry felt the blade slice the skin on his neck. It bit deep, the curve of the blade cutting through veins and tendons like butter. He felt a gush of arterial spray escape him. It sounded like a tap being turned on. The coppery aroma of blood mingled with the stench of rotting flesh. Her left hand stifled his screams as her right repeatedly slashed with the blade. Jerry dropped to his knees and drank from the spraying artery. The woman joined him and lapped greedily at the blood. Barry prayed for unconsciousness, but the pain didn't stop for a long time after his body was still. The pain stayed with him as he drifted into a burning black eternity.

44 Brick St. The Police investigation and following events as I understand them...

DI ANNIE JONES STEPPED under the crime scene tape which cordoned off the road and the front of number 44.

'Can you tell us what's going on, Inspector?' a journalist shouted from across the road. She recognised him and two others as local paparazzi. His name was Jez Felling, and he was an arsehole of the first degree. Two uniformed officers looked cold and extremely unhappy to be policing the cordon. The rain had been drizzling relentlessly since they had arrived on the scene and there was no let up.

'Good afternoon, Jez. You probably know more about what's going on than me at the moment,' she answered with a nod. Ignoring them was never good for public relations. She had encountered Jez several times and she found that if she was civil with him, he wasn't quite as scathing with his assessment of their investigations. He obviously had an informer in the uniformed division, because he seemed to arrive at the scene of suspected murders before the detectives that were despatched to the scene. Backhanders were common in the Instagram world that we live in.

'I'll be making a statement later, as soon as we know what we're dealing with and have a handle on it.'

'Thanks, Inspector.' He appeared to be happy. Annie thought that she had got away lightly until he shouted to her again. 'Could you give us a comment on the satanic slant to the murder?'

Annie opened her mouth to speak but the words wouldn't come out. Someone had given him far too many details. It was something that they wanted to keep a lid on but that wouldn't be possible now. She was taken aback by the bluntness of his question although she knew that they would come eventually.

'That's a matter for the investigation to decide. We don't know what the motive is yet, so please don't jump to any conclusions yet, Jez,' she mumbled. 'I don't have any more to say just yet but if I find out who is feeding you confidential information, they'll be directing traffic for the next ten years.'

'Could it be connected to the Father Thomas case?'

She put her head down and walked towards a CSI officer who was processing a Ford Focus twenty metres away. She blushed red with anger.

Annie did have an opinion, but it wasn't for general consumption. She had been dealing with the rumours of a satanic cult in the city for a lot longer than her colleagues and associates had. For them, this was just another murder. Yes, it was a shock and one they would talk about over a pint after work. For her it was awkward to see other people's reaction. No one took it seriously. It was a standing joke, but she didn't find it funny. Annie had spent hours in the office piecing snippets of information together. Having said all that, the bluntness of the question had made her feel uncomfortable to say the least. The cat was out of the bag on this one. Wounds were still raw following the death of the paedophile priest, Father Thomas, and victims had spoken of satanic rituals being part of the abuse. Any connection to that investigation would fuel a press frenzy. She was fully aware that Father Thomas had been seen at 44 Brick Street on the day of his death. Jez Felling hadn't made the connection yet, but he would. There was no doubt about it.

The Ford was parked across the road from number 44 and there was nothing unremarkable about. It had been established that the parties had arrived in separate vehicles.

'Anything out of the ordinary?' Annie asked.

'Nothing to report,' the CSI said, without looking up. He looked cold and wet.

She decided to go straight inside, before picking up any minor details from the vehicle later. The giant frame of her Detective Sergeant, Jim Stirling, appeared in the doorway. His expression was rarely summery, but it was particularly grim that day. He wrinkled his nose in disgust.

'I hope you've brought your eucalyptus, Guv,' he grunted as she reached the stone steps, which led up to the door. 'This is a very wet one.'

'Your descriptive powers never cease to amaze me,' she grinned. Jim Stirling appeared to have been repeatedly smacked in the face with a spade when he was a child. His nose was flattened and bent from an amateur boxing career as a teenager. He looked like he was built from an oak tree and his wit was dark and cutting. 'Wet doesn't sound good.'

'There isn't a word for this one, Guv.' Stirling stepped aside to let her into the hallway. 'You will get the impression immediately.' He pointed to the floor and far wall which she could see from outside before stepping in. She took a small jar from her pocket and smeared the eucalyptus balm beneath her nostrils. 'I think the attack started here.'

Annie stepped inside, and the chill struck her immediately. Stirling saw the startled expression on her face.

'It's like a fridge in here,' he commented. 'Gets colder the further inside you go.'

Annie shivered and looked around. Her detective's brain was analysing everything in detail. Stirling knew the drill. Annie Jones didn't appreciate too much information until she asked for it. She liked to work things out for herself. Her first impressions were what made her a standout DI.

'Is Kathy Brooks here yet?' she asked, kneeling next to the wall where she had spotted a dent in the damp plaster. A blood smear ran from the dent to the skirting board and what appeared to be fragments of teeth lay in a pool of congealed blood. Insects were feeding on the sticky mess. 'The cockroaches are feasting on our evidence here.'

'I wouldn't worry about it too much.' Kathy spoke from the other room. She peered around the door frame and smiled beneath her mask. Annie could tell that she was smiling by the way her eyes crinkled at the corners. 'There's plenty of our victim around the house. If they eat a bit, there's more. To be honest, it would take me a month of Sundays to recover all of him.'

'Rage killing?' Annie frowned.

'Looking at the hallway in isolation, I would say that's a possibility but come in here,' Kathy beckoned with a gloved hand. 'In here is a different story.' She disappeared back into the other room.

Annie took another look around the hallway before squeezing past Stirling into the doorway.

'Jesus,' she said beneath her breath.

'Nope, Jesus hasn't been here,' Stirling said gruffly. 'He is on the other side.'

'Our victim is Barry Bishop,' Kathy said, walking around the eviscerated remains of a man. Annie could tell that he was a man because his face appeared to be reasonably undamaged, and the breasts were those of a male. 'His jugular was slashed with a sharp weapon, which would explain the arterial spray in the hallway. Then he was carried in here and placed into the middle of this circle,' she said, pointing to the floor. A circle had been scraped into the rotting debris which covered the floor, and a nine-angled star was carved inside the circle. Dirt and grime, moss and fungus had formed a living carpet on the wooden floorboards. Thick church candles formed a larger circle concentric to the first. Annie could see symbols and words written in the dirt. They meant nothing to her.

'Here, he was stripped, disembowelled and his genitals were removed. I haven't found them yet. Death was exsanguination.'

'This is some kind of satanic ritual,' Annie said. 'Jez Felling is outside, and he asked about the satanic slant to the murder.'

'That man is a maggot,' Stirling grunted. 'How the fuck does he know that?'

'You tell me,' Annie said. 'Someone is feeding him with information, which we know happens, but if that hits the news, we're going to have a shitstorm to deal with.'

She walked around the room staying close to the walls. She wanted to view the scene from every possible angle.

'It's definitely a ritual killing,' Annie said.

'It looks that way, although I'm no expert,' Kathy shrugged.

'I've sent photographs of the symbols back to the office,' Stirling said. 'Smithy is researching them now and cross-checking them with anything similar with the other divisions.'

'Is he looking at the Father Thomas case too?' Annie asked. Stirling nodded. 'Good,' Annie said nodding. 'There are two sets of male clothing here and four shoes?'

'Our suspect was found naked, Guv,' Stirling explained.

'Have we got a name?' Annie asked.

'Jerry Bracknall, age twenty-two, no record at all. Not even a speeding fine. Apparently, he walked into the estate agent where Bishop worked this morning. They showed him the details for this place. He asked to view it and when they got here, he turned psycho.'

'This isn't a random killing,' Annie said. 'This was staged and well planned.'

'He could have brought all this paraphernalia with him?' Stirling said.

'It's possible but that doesn't match the murder,' Annie said doubtfully. 'He couldn't have carried out a frenzied attack on this scale and then arranged the scene after.'

'This circle and star were here before this happened,' Kathy said, shaking her head. 'I agree that this was planned before the victim arrived here.'

'Check with the estate agents to see if he had a haversack or holdall with him.'

'Guv.'

Annie looked at Stirling and shrugged.

'This is too detailed to be random.' She walked around the circle again. 'So, Jerry Bracknall just walked into an estate agent and asked for a viewing, so that he could perform some kind of satanic ceremony on the poor unfortunate who accompanied him?'

'Not according to Jerry Bracknall.' Stirling shook his head as he spoke. He referred to his notebook. 'Bracknall claims that when they arrived there was a naked woman beneath the stairs. She was covered in 'writing', he said.'

'A naked lady waiting in an empty house, covered in writing?'

'That's what he said, Guv, although he was a gibbering idiot to be honest. He claims not to have been involved at all.'

'So, he watched a man being butchered and didn't help, or didn't run out of the front door?'

'Pretty much what I said to him, but he became quite irate and upset that I thought he could be involved.' Stirling shook his head as he spoke. 'He was clearly mentally disturbed and rambling, and he couldn't explain why the first officers on the scene found him sitting between the victim's legs with his intestines wrapped around his neck like a scarf.'

'I am feeling an insanity plea coming here,' Annie said.

'He claims to have no idea what happened, but he denies killing him. According to him, the woman killed him, and he blanked out. When he woke up, he was naked and covered in blood and the police were handcuffing him.'

'That's a convenient blackout, don't you think?'

'Absolutely.'

'Have we checked if he has any mental health issues on record?'

'Nothing has been flagged up, but we're still digging through his records, Guv.'

'Has he been sectioned?'

'He's being processed now.'

'What do you think?'

'I spoke to him in the van, Guv.' Stirling shrugged and grimaced. 'He didn't look high or drunk, but he was talking complete shite. There were bits which were lucid, but the rest was gobbledegook. I think they'll section him.'

'Great,' Annie sighed. 'And I don't suppose the responding officers saw a naked woman covered in writing?'

'No, Guv.'

'He said the woman came from beneath the stairs. Did they search beneath the stairs?' Annie asked looking back into the hallway. The wooden panelling looked warped and disc-shaped mushrooms grew in clusters along the skirting boards.

'Not yet,' Stirling said shaking his head. 'There's no obvious cellar door.'

'Houses of this age tend to have the doors shaped into the panelling.'

'That was my guess too,' Stirling agreed. 'They cleared the upper floors first. There was no obvious sign of anyone else being here, so they isolated the crime scene and waited for us. I was waiting for you before I go exploring. Do you want to wait for backup?'

'I've got you to look after me. I think we'll be fine, don't you?'

'I'll look for a cellar door,' Stirling said walking back into the hall. The staircase ran up the right-hand side, climbing to a landing before twisting to the left, where it joined the first floor. Stirling rapped on the panelling with his huge fist. The wood felt spongy and rotten beneath his knuckles. He pushed on the panels with his palms, and they creaked beneath his considerable weight. The panels to his left sounded hollow. He pressed them again and released the pressure quickly. The hidden panel clicked open, and a blast of foul-smelling air rushed up from the blackness to meet him. Stirling recoiled as if an invisible fist had punched him on the nose.

'We have a door, Guv,' he called to the front room. He tested the staircase with a size thirteen boot. It groaned but held beneath his bulk. 'It's like a rose garden up here compared to the stink down there. Something has died down here,' he moaned, as he ducked into the cellar.

Annie grabbed a torch and handed it to him. He took it and wafted it around to illuminate the area at the bottom of the steps. The floor looked dry, paved with concrete slabs. They were a mishmash of shapes, colours and sizes. Stirling couldn't see any sign of a naked woman waiting to pounce. He descended three more steps and ducked beneath the roof, using the torch to see the entire cellar. The smell was overwhelming, and he covered his nose with one huge hand. He looked around and shook his head in disbelief.

'What is it?' Annie asked anxiously.

'You need to see this for yourself.'

They walked down to the bottom of the steps and looked up.

Every inch of the exposed joists and floorboards, which formed the ceiling of the cellar, were hidden by the dangling carcasses of rats, cats and dogs, which were nailed to the ceiling, their teeth fixed in permanent snarls. The floor at the centre of the room seemed to writhe, an undulating mass of maggots. Annie nearly balked. The sight combined with the stench were too much for her constitution. As she took in the scene, she realised that the walls were daubed with words, thousands upon thousands of lines of script written in a language which she couldn't decipher in her mind. The words seemed to drift and change shape and the walls pulsated. They appeared to swell and buzz and rush towards her. She thought she was hallucinating, until a swarm of bloated flies took off simultaneously and the world turned to black.

ANNIE WAVED HER ARMS wildly, but a tsunami of flies swamped her. She felt them bouncing off her skin and crawling into her ears and nostrils. Their spiked little legs scratched at the tender skin up her nose and became tangled in her hair. She dared not scream. Opening her mouth would be suicide. They would choke her within seconds. Annie staggered blindly, searching for a space where she could breathe and open her eyes. Her lungs began to burn, desperate for fresh air. Disorientation gripped her, and she staggered about blindly. She could feel floor beneath her feet moving. She sensed, rather than heard, hundreds of tiny maggots bursting with each step. The squelching beneath her shoes, the deafening noise, the stench, the blindness and the inability to breathe through her nose or mouth was too much. She felt her knees buckle and she knew that if she fell, she probably wouldn't rise. An invisible weight tried to force her down. She felt icy hands clawing at her, pulling at her, dragging her towards the writhing rotting slime.

'*Give in, Annie, surrender to decay.*'

Something urged her to succumb to the darkness. It wasn't a voice that she could hear. It was a suggestion; a powerful urge to give up.

'*Open your mouth and let the filth overwhelm you. Once the initial panic of suffocation is over, you will find peace in the chaos. Let it happen, Annie, just let it happen, Annie.*'

'Annie!' She heard another voice. Not the ones in her head. 'Annie!'

Strong hands grabbed her, and she was swept off her feet. She felt herself being dragged backwards sharply. Her coat ripped beneath the pressure. Suddenly, she was lifted off her feet and carried roughly up the lower steps. As she was carried her nostrils cleared a little and she sneezed and forced bluebottles and house flies from her airways. She still couldn't open her mouth as the swarm engulfed them.

'Move!'

She heard Stirling growl. He roared like a wounded bull, and she felt him climbing the steps out of the cellar. She couldn't hear anything but the buzzing of millions of wings. Stirling stumbled, and she was flung forward. Her shin scraped against the steps and then he was up and moving towards fresh air again. His massive legs pumped, the muscles burning with oxygen starvation and lactic acid. They burst out of the cellar door and Annie felt the swarm dissipate. Stirling didn't stop until they were out of the house and halfway across the road. He dropped to his knees and dumped Annie unceremoniously onto the tarmac.

She spluttered and sucked air into her lungs, still swatting at the flies which clung to her face. Annie felt hands on her, helping hands. She opened her eyes to see a paramedic team and uniformed officers helping them. Kathy Brooks was lying on her back coughing and spluttering. Her white forensic suit was covered with crawling black flies. Stirling was on his hands and knees, heaving the contents of his stomach onto the road. Annie heard it splatter and although it was disgusting, it was nothing to where they had been. She slapped at the insects which were caught in her hair, fighting the urge to scream and panic.

'Are you okay?' a paramedic asked.

'Yes,' Annie croaked. 'I'm okay. Sort him out,' she nodded towards Stirling. She was well aware that he had saved her. 'Stop being sick on the road, you big oaf,' Annie said to him. 'You'll be on the front page of the Echo tomorrow,' she added, pointing towards the reporters. They were clicking away with their digital cameras and chatting excitedly about what they had just witnessed. Jim Stirling sat back on his heels and looked in their direction.

'I can see the headlines, 'MIT detectives can't stomach the job',' she added, joking, although she didn't laugh. It was her way of ignoring what had just happened. 'They'll have a field day coming up with a caption.'

'How about MIT detective inserts Nikon camera up reporter's arse?' he replied spitting onto the road. 'Sorry about that but I hate flies. I swallowed a few of the horrible little bastards.'

'No problem,' Annie smiled thinly. 'And thank you. I wasn't doing well down there.'

19.00-PM
 44 Brick Street

ANNIE WANDERED THROUGH the ground floor as a
small army of CSI processed the terraced house. A constant
stream of uniformed officers ferried the decomposing evidence
from the cellar in sealed plastic bags. Although it was not as
powerful, the choking stench lingered.

'What are we looking for?' Annie asked herself. The entire
scene was like something from a poorly-made horror flick. Or
was she reading too much into it? Was Bracknall an isolated
lunatic who had planned a complicated murder over months?
If that was all the case had to it, then it was solved.

Something about the house told her that wasn't the entire
truth. She turned around and saw Kathy staring at an
ornamental fireplace in what passed for the living room. It was
tiny and wouldn't take more than a settee and a couple of
chairs. It had a window which overlooked the back yard, and
it connected the kitchen to the rest of the house. Everywhere
was dust and cobwebs, but the fireplace stood out as being
too decorative and out of keeping with the rest of the house.
Although it was covered in grime, there wasn't a speck of
damage to it anywhere. The side panels depicted two
pre-Raphaelite angels being tortured by hell-fire. A

beautifully-detailed demon had speared them with a pitchfork-like implement and held them over the flames. Annie had an interest in carvings and sculpture, but she had never seen anything like it before. She couldn't decide if it was a depiction of Dante or something else. The light reflected from the marble; the colours were so vivid they almost reflected off the opposite walls like prisms.

'This is one of the most amazing carvings I've ever seen,' Annie commented flatly. 'What the hell is it doing in here?' she mused. 'How is it possible that this has survived and never been sold or stolen?'

Kathy gave a nervous cough. 'Beats me. It's not my sort of thing,' she said, not very convincingly. 'Do you think it's valuable?'

'These Victorian fireplaces were being snapped up by developers for a small fortune before the virus and most of them were mass produced. I would say that it is unique,' Annie said. 'And bearing in mind the occult theme of the murder, I think that this address was chosen for a specific reason, not just because it's an empty property.'

Kathy eyed her quizzically. 'There's something you're not saying, isn't there?' She tilted her head and frowned. 'We've worked together too long to fob me off, Annie.'

'I don't know what you're driving at.' Annie raised her eyebrows. 'It's as much a puzzle to me as it is to you, Dr Brooks.'

'Well, it stinks in here but now I can smell bullshit too!' Kathy whispered and put a finger to her lips. 'You can tell me what you think.'

'Okay, let's start with what we've found here. Look at the cellar,' Annie shrugged. 'There must have been hundreds of animals nailed to the ceiling. That was months, if not years of work. Put it all together, the dead animals, the scripture on the walls. Then look at this fireplace, and tell me it's all a coincidence?'

'Not a chance.'

'So, did Jerry Bracknall set this up so that he could bring Bishop here, or was he an innocent victim who stumbled into this?'

'I just process the evidence left behind.' Kathy shivered visibly. 'But there's something about this house. It's not right.'

'I get that feeling too.'

'Any ideas on the bare footprints near to the victim?'

Annie was grasping for something to explain Jerry Bracknall's version of events. Not that it made sense anyway but if they could prove the existence of the woman, it could explain who created the pet cemetery in the cellar. 'I know it's early days, but we need to get a grip of this before I start getting questions from upstairs?'

'There are footprints but the floor is covered in moss. The damp has made everything spongy. Once we get the body moved, I'll be able to distinguish between them.'

'Okay.' Annie grimaced. 'When are you going to move him?'

She took a closer look at the fireplace, fascinated by the detail. The choking sensation of the swarm returned instantly, and a blinding white light flashed in her mind. She staggered backwards and gasped.

'Jesus!'

'What's up, Guv?' Stirling's gruff voice came from behind her. He had been checking the kitchen and tiny backyard. 'Are you okay?'

'I just had a dizzy moment,' Annie said, staring at the fireplace. 'This bloody place has got me spooked.'

She composed herself and stepped back closer to the fireplace. There was no way she was going to be intimidated by a slab of marble. She reached out and touched the tortured expression of an angel's face. Its mouth was twisted in agony. Her eyes were drawn to the hearth.

'Look here.' She pointed as she spoke. She stepped back and stood close to Stirling. 'Can you see that?'

The three of them stared at the floorboards in front of the hearth. They were bare wood for twelve inches before the carpet of moss and mould began. The angles were straight and clear. 'Mother Nature doesn't grow in straight lines. I don't think these boards were covered with a hearth rug, do you?'

Stirling knelt on one knee and looked at the side of the hearth. There were score lines in the wood. Leaning across he checked the other side.

'There are scratches in the floorboards here, look. Something very heavy has been dragged.'

'Is the hearth attached to the fireplace?' Kathy asked.

'I don't think so,' Stirling said tugging at the slate hearth. He grunted as his sinews tightened and his hands gripped the smooth stone. The hearth moved an inch from the base of the fireplace. He looked between the gap. 'Could you get me some light, please?'

Kathy went into the front room and returned with a torch. She handed it to Annie who held it over the hearth. Stirling heaved again, and it slid across the wood until the edge met the moss carpet. The torchlight illuminated a rectangular hole beneath the fireplace. Stirling looked around at Annie and their eyes met for a moment, confusion in both.

'Let's get some pictures of this before we move it.'

The yellowed skull of a ram was on top of a book. The ram had four horns, two on each side, which curled twice to the tips. The teeth were those of a carnivore, sharp incisors lined the jawbone. The book beneath it was a thousand pages thick at least. It was covered and bound with a human face, the skin tanned to leather. The eyes and lips had been stitched with leather thread and the nose had been flattened to the right. Gold lettering embossed the cover, written in script that none of them recognised.

'Just when you think you have seen it all.' Annie turned to Kathy. The expression on Kathy's face said that she agreed.

'Do you think it's real?' Kathy asked.

'In this house, absolutely.'

21.00-PM 44 BRICK STREET

'THERE'S A GENTLEMEN called Arthur Cross at the cordon, Guv,' a uniformed officer called into the hallway. 'He says that you're expecting him?'

Annie peered around the living room door and waved her hand.

'Ask him to come in,' she shouted. The hallway was still busy with CSI officers clearing the cellar. She wasn't sure what to expect. Arthur Cross had been recommended by her senior officer, Superintendent Alec Ramsay, who had used him to advise the department on a string of ritual murders some years before. He said that he was a strange man but that when it came to the occult, he knew his stuff. She caught sight of a well-dressed man in his fifties, wearing a pale grey suit. He stepped into the house, and she watched the expression on his face change dramatically.

'Funny how this place does that to you,' she thought. It was almost reassuring to see that it wasn't just her that felt the change in temperature when they entered the building, although Annie was convinced that it wasn't just the temperature that people sensed. There was something else too. Arthur Cross stood rooted to the floor just inside the doorway while a steady stream of white-clad officers filed past him as if he wasn't there. His eyes were closed, and he seemed to be reciting something.

'I hope he's not praying,' Annie muttered to herself. 'Please don't let him be praying. I do not need the god squad here right now.' She stepped into the hallway.

'Hello Mr Cross.' She spoke loudly. His eyes opened widely, and he looked at her. His gaze was instantly drawn to her eyes. 'I'm DI Jones.'

She offered her hand, and he shook it firmly. His eyes were steely grey, sharp and bright. He seemed to look into her. His greying blond hair was cropped tightly to his head.

'My Christian name is Arthur, Inspector.' He walked towards the living room and looked around. His eyes darted everywhere. 'Please, call me Arthur.'

'Thanks for coming at such short notice, Arthur,' she smiled. He looked past her into the room, his piercing eyes analysing the scene. His attention was drawn to the nine-angled star on the floor. He looked concerned by it. For reasons that she couldn't explain, his presence was somewhat reassuring to her. The oppressive atmosphere in the house had lifted slightly. 'My senior officer recommended you to me.'

'How is Alec?' he asked politely. Annie could sense that he was impatient to see the scene. He glanced at her, but his attention was drawn to the living room.

'He's winding down to retirement,' Annie said. 'I asked for your help because there are some items that we have found which we need help to identify.' She cut to the chase. 'Would you look at them and tell us what we're dealing with?'

'Of course,' he nodded. 'Please show me.' He gestured to the room eagerly. They stepped inside, and she leaned against the wall and folded her arms while he studied the markings. He looked at the circle of candles which surrounded the Sigil and the script and then he studied the symbols. His hand stroked his chin as he studied them. Annie noticed that his hands were strong, and his wrists were thick and muscular. He wasn't a tall man, but he was solidly built. The suit disguised a powerful physique.

'Oh dear, oh dear, oh dear,' he muttered, shaking his head. His brow furrowed with deep wrinkles, which accentuated the jagged scars on his scalp. He looked up into her eyes and his glare startled her. 'Ice axe.'

'I beg your pardon?'

'The scars that you are looking at on my head were caused by an ice axe.'

'I didn't mean to stare,' Annie stuttered, feeling even more like he could see inside her mind. 'I won't ask what happened.'

'Best not to, unless you want me to lie to you.' He grinned, and his eyes glinted. The smile disappeared as a thought occurred. 'Did your victim have his genitals removed?'

'Yes.' Annie raised her eyebrows. Stirling stood in the doorway listening. His eyes caught hers at Arthur's intuitive question. 'How did you know that the victim was male?'

'It is written in the script.' He pointed to the floorboards. 'Some rituals are gender specific, and some are not. This one is.'

'I see,' Annie said looking at Stirling who didn't seem impressed.

'Was he disembowelled?'

'Yes.'

'Oh dear.'

He shook his head again. Arthur sighed and crossed the room. He looked around at the blood-stained floor. 'Are the genitals missing?'

'We haven't found them yet.'

'You won't find them,' Arthur said, matter-of-factly.

'Why?'

'They would have been consumed during the ceremony,' he said frowning.

'Consumed?' Stirling asked, confused. He couldn't pin down where the expert's accent was from, but he wasn't local. 'What do you mean?'

'They would have been eaten as part of the ceremony,' Arthur explained casually. 'The genitals are removed and eaten in front of the victim, preferably while they are still alive.' He paused. 'It heightens their terror, which in turn draws more of the 'accusal' or dark energy into the room where the ceremony is being held.'

'Accusal?' Annie asked.

'It is dark energy as opposed to good energy and they believe that they can draw the energy to them by performing certain rituals and ceremonies.'

'And you know that they were doing this ceremony, because?' Stirling asked, even more confused.

'Because Christmas is coming,' Arthur said nonchalantly. 'Christmas and Easter are important dates in the satanic calendar, just as they are for Christians. For practising Christians those dates are about Jesus, but for most people they are about presents and turkey and about chocolate eggs, but it is also a major event on the Satanic calendar.' He smiled. 'To mock Jesus Christ, a man is sacrificed, disembowelled, and his genitals are removed and eaten before his eyes. This is followed by three days of fasting and chanting the demonic rites.'

'Of course, it is.' Stirling rolled his eyes. 'Three days of chanting. Silly me for not thinking of that.' He sighed and shook his head. 'Fasting and chanting. We need to put out an alert on anyone who is chanting and looks hungry.'

Arthur looked at the big detective sharply. He pointed his index finger at him and wagged it like a teacher scolding a naughty schoolboy.

'What you need to do, is listen to what I am about to tell you with an open mind, otherwise there is no point in my being here.' He looked to Annie as he spoke. 'Inspector, please don't assume that I hold any stay in these teachings because whether I do or I don't is of no consequence,' he said, looking back at Stirling sternly. 'What does matter, is that your killer absolutely believes in what she is doing. She is following the teachings of her religion, just as a priest or rabbi would theirs.' He tapped his open palm with his fist to reinforce every word. 'Totally, completely, absolutely, steadfastly and unreservedly believes that what she is doing will take her to the next level of the Satanic hierarchy.' He smiled and shook his head. 'It is a religion just like any other. Is it so difficult to believe?'

'Wait a minute. You said the killer is female?' Stirling asked.

'This ceremony is performed by a female to enhance her powers and make her stronger,' Arthur said.

'There was no female here.'

'You asked me to explain what you have found and I'm explaining it to you.'

'No offence meant but it is pushing the boundary of my imagination, to be honest.'

'You saw men flying jets into the Twin Towers, didn't you?' Arthur asked.

'Of course,' Stirling shrugged. 'I don't see the connection.'

'They did what they did for their beliefs, to reach a better place when they died. This is her way of achieving the same thing. She will do whatever it takes for her belief, and this is the important thing, which you must remember.' He paused. 'She will enjoy every second of it. Your murderer will keep on killing.'

'Why are you so sure it's she?' Annie asked. 'Explain that bit to me.'

'This circle, the goat head marked on the floor and the symbols around it make up what is called the 'Sigil of Baphomet'. She is the female devil, the dark Goddess, and this ceremony must be orchestrated by a female who has already climbed to a position of authority within the dark church. It can only be conducted by a High Priestess.'

'High Priestess,' Stirling repeated flatly.

Annie and Stirling exchanged glances. Annie shook her head imperceptibly to warn him to shut up and to keep his cynicism to himself.

'We found a suspect here at the scene,' Annie explained. 'He was naked and covered with the victim's intestines, but he claims that he had nothing to do with the murder. He says that there was a naked woman in the house when they arrived and that she was covered in 'writing'.'

'This is bad. It's very bad.' Arthur rubbed his chin again. 'Only the genuine exponents of the left-hand path could do this. It is a power attained by only a few.'

'I don't understand.'

'Some people play at this for the thrill of being a Devil worshiper when it suits them. Like a Christian who goes to church for weddings and funerals only, but there are real practitioners too. This woman is the real thing, and she is very dangerous indeed.' He paused. 'Let me try to explain this to you without you thinking that I'm bat-shit crazy. I have studied the dark arts for many years and this ceremony is something I have only read about. The Priestess would have prepared the altar for months.' He looked at Annie as he spoke. 'She chose this place because this act must be carried out over 'death'. The more death in the vicinity, the greater the effect of the ceremony.' Arthur paused. 'There will be dead animals somewhere in the house. Lots of them.'

'I am sure that you could guess that from the smell. The place reeks of decomposition,' Stirling shrugged. 'There are dead animals in the cellar below us.' Stirling frowned. 'So, that is why they killed all those animals?'

'Yes. Their death, and subsequent decay, add to the power. That is what they believe.'

There are hundreds of dead animals down there,' Annie said. 'Dogs, cats, rodents, even some birds and a couple of foxes I believe.' Annie nodded. 'Hundreds of them nailed to the rafters beneath this room. So, that is Satanic?'

Arthur shook his head and held up a hand. 'No, no, no,' he said excitedly. 'The dead animals are something else entirely. They are part of another ceremony completely. That is Witchcraft which accentuates the evil. They work hand in hand sometimes.'

'You said the altar had to be above the dead?' Stirling said.

'Yes, I did, three thousand six hundred and fifty-one dead people to be precise,' Arthur explained.

'Dead people?' Annie said. 'What are you talking about?'

'A mass grave was discovered here in the seventies, thousands of graves lie beneath this area. Many theories were put forward, plague pits, ethnic cleansing by the locals, but the truth is that the bodies were found buried beneath this street in coffins, laid in a big square. There were reports of holes in the skulls and stakes between the ribs.'

'Now you're pushing it,' Stirling scoffed.

'It is true, but I didn't click that it was here,' Annie interrupted. 'I've read about it before in a local history book. They were building a school when they found the burial ground. It caused an outcry and the local council tried to hush it up and needed to dispose of the bodies quickly. Ancient maps indicated that there may have been a graveyard here which allegedly was cleared when the houses were built.'

'You're right, Inspector. But I have evidence from workers at the site who claimed that the contractors had cleared the headstones but left the coffins in situ to save money.'

'I read that some were removed and when they dug them up, they took them to the crematorium.' She grimaced. 'Urban myth says that the coffins wouldn't burn.'

'That is correct,' Arthur said. 'That is why they picked this area for their ceremonies. Thousands of the dead are beneath these streets. The animals were just an enhancement. They helped to focus the energy beneath this room, but the real dark energy is beneath us. Thousands of dead people lying in desecrated graves.'

'Carry on, please,' Annie said.

Arthur looked thoughtful and paced up and down looking at the symbols.

'Sacrifice preparation is as important as the act itself, but this is just the pre-Christmas ceremony. It is a precursor to the main event.' He raised his finger again. 'This is part of the build-up to the Da Muer Ritual, which is the rape, torture and sacrifice of a woman and young girl, preferably related, but that too is just part of the lead into Walpurgis or Beltane Rituals.'

'This is baffling my head,' Stirling said.

'I'm sure it is,' Arthur said. 'But these people are deeply religious, and those dates are sacrosanct to them. They involve multiple sacrifices. I'm afraid that from what I can see here, the Priestess who carried out this ceremony knows exactly what she is doing, and this is just the start. There will be more killed in the next few months.'

'Okay. Let's say we take this seriously; will the victims be picked at random?' Stirling asked.

'She has her sacrifices selected and marked,' Arthur nodded. 'Looking at the detail she has used here, there's no doubt in my mind that she knows exactly who they will be. So do her followers.'

'Followers?' Stirling grumbled.

'She is not working alone.' Arthur shook his head. 'Anyone who can channel this much evil is near the top of the tree.' He held his hands up to the ceiling. 'You can feel it as soon as you walk into the house. She has minions, no doubt about it, and a lot of the time their sacrifices are chosen from within the group. Most initiates never make their own full initiation. They are culled. Once the sinister tribe is certain that the initiate will not be missed, they are used in a ceremony.'

'So, they kill their own?' Annie asked.

He shrugged. 'Yes. This is a religion of evil. It keeps their secrets intact and provides a steady stream of victims. Either way, they will bring her victims to her. They feed her like ants in a nest feeding the queen.'

Annie folded her arms and looked at the Sigil while she processed the information. She felt a shiver run down her spine. Stirling looked flushed as if he had been slapped across the face.

'Could our suspect be telling the truth?' Annie asked.

'That he was not involved, you mean?' Arthur frowned.

'Yes,' Stirling said. 'He says that he has no memory of the murder.'

'Have his stomach pumped.'

'What?'

'If he ate your victim's genitals during the ceremony, then it was an initiation as well as a sacrifice,' Arthur shrugged. 'If he didn't, then the Priestess did but I'm certain your suspect was a willing participant although he may not have realised what he was getting himself involved in.'

Stirling shook his head in disbelief. He took out his mobile and speed dialed the station.

'Can we get his stomach pumped if he's been sectioned?'

Annie shrugged and frowned.

'We're looking for evidence in a murder case and he may have eaten the victim. I suppose so.'

She looked at Arthur and gestured to the doorway.

'I wonder if you could look at this room for me, please,' Annie said, breaking an uncomfortable silence. Arthur Cross talked as if he was explaining the rules of a board game. He seemed blissfully unaware of the impact his information had on those who were ignorant to the occult.

'You have been very helpful already, but can I ask you to take a look in here?'

Annie walked out of the room and into the smaller living room. Arthur followed her, his eyes absorbing every detail.

'This fireplace seems to have a demonic theme, wouldn't you agree?'

'I would indeed,' Arthur said excitedly. 'The carvings are beautiful.'

'Coincidence?'

'No.' He shook his head. 'Whoever had it built also had a sense of the darkness which dwells beneath this house.' His role as the librarian of an occult bookshop had gifted him an almost unlimited amount of reference material. 'I have only ever seen pictures of this carving online. This is a carving of a lost painting by Hieronymus Bosch. Nobody knows where it is.' He looked at Annie to gauge her understanding of the artist. She appeared to understand. 'You're familiar with his works?'

'I much prefer Goya's dark stuff, but I love The Pit.'

'Then you will realise that this fireplace was commissioned by someone who had a deep love of the left-hand path.' He touched the marble and Annie saw him flinch visibly just as she had earlier. 'It has its own electricity doesn't it!'

He touched it again and let his fingers explore the smooth detail of the demon's face. 'Incredible work. It must be worth a fortune.'

'We found these hidden beneath the fireplace.' Annie pointed to the windowsill as she spoke. 'This ram's skull and a book wrapped in human skin.' She felt her eyes drawn to the leather face. 'Have you ever seen anything like this?'

'Oh yes. There are many books bound in human skin.' He frowned, looking at the skull. 'The skull is that of a Jacob sheep. The multi-horned breed goes back in records found in the Sumerian cities of ancient Uruk, in around 3000 BC. They have always been connected to mysticism and the occult, Inspector, centuries before anybody depicted Satan as a horned being.'

'What about the teeth?' Annie pointed to the incisors. 'I haven't seen any herbivores with teeth like this.'

'They have been added long after the poor animal stopped bleating,' Arthur said smiling. He bent over to inspect the teeth closely. 'Super glue I suspect.'

'That's a relief,' Annie joked. 'I was beginning to think that we had slipped into the twilight zone.'

'Unfortunately, it visits us sometimes, Inspector.'

'And the book,' she shrugged. 'Please tell me that is a fake too.'

Arthur touched the spine with his index finger. 'Have you fingerprinted it?' He turned to Annie.

'Yes.'

'This is the real thing. I have several books covered and bound with skin, in my shop.'

'You're kidding me?' Stirling loomed behind them, having finished his phone call.

'The skull has fake teeth, but the book is real.' She brought him up to speed.

'The practice of binding books in human skin, known as anthropodermic bibliopegy, is not just the stuff of dark legends and horror fiction,' Arthur said, touching the sewn lips. 'It was a real technique which, although frowned upon and considered ghastly by today's standards, was officially practiced since the 17th century but there are examples from much earlier.'

He looked at their faces to test their reaction. Annie looked horrified, whereas her sergeant looked skeptical.

'The technique was used to bind such texts as anatomy books, last will and testaments and judicial proceedings.' He paused and smiled. 'Of course, there have been many legends concerning this practice, almost all of which have cast it in an evil light. But anthropodermic bibliopegy has a distinct history of being utilized for regular, and even mundane, texts. This, however, is far from mundane. This book is as evil as evil can be.'

'Whose face is that?' Annie asked.

'I have seen the use of the facial skin before,' Arthur said, pointing to the book. 'There is a book which is a recollection of the failure and subsequent arrest and execution of the Gunpowder Plotters. Guy Fawkes and his crew.' He wagged his finger and smiled. 'The leader of the conspirators was Father Henry Garnet, the head of the Jesuits in England. It was his flesh which was used after his execution to bind their book. The book has a Latin inscription on its cover which, when translated, reads: 'Severe penitence punished the flesh.' This is one of the most famous examples of anthropodermic bibliopegy since many believe that you can see the Father's face, forever twisted in agony, on its cover.' He pointed to the book on the windowsill. 'This example, however, leaves us in no doubt that the face was used. The answer to your question as to whose face it is lies within the pages.'

'What the hell is it about?' Stirling asked.

'What the 'hell' is very apt, Sergeant.' Arthur opened the cover and followed the bizarre text inside with his finger. He turned a page, studied it, and then turned another. He shook his head slowly and sighed. 'It is Luciferian Witchcraft.'

'Witchcraft?' Annie repeated staring at the leathered face.

'Witchcraft?' Stirling scoffed. 'Like a book of spells?'

'I don't think that you should mock what you don't understand.'

'We didn't find a broomstick, maybe she escaped on it.' Stirling shrugged. 'Sorry. I can't help myself.'

'And if she had a black cat, then she nailed it to the ceiling in the cellar?' Arthur smirked. 'The authors of this collection were all witches but are long since dead.' Arthur ignored the big detective's cynicism. 'This is a huge compendium of shocking rituals such as the one you witnessed today. To be clear, and to put things into perspective, that is one of the tamer ceremonies which can be used for advancement.' He turned some pages and pointed to a heading. 'This script is a tranche of Magick Hebrew used by the exponents of the left-hand traditions when they write books.'

'Why that language in particular?' Annie asked.

'Because it's so difficult to master.'

'I don't follow.'

'One has to have an elevated level of intelligence to be able to learn, read and understand the text,' he explained in hushed tones. 'It puts some safeguards in place so that should the manuscript fall into the wrong hands, it could not be used for the wrong reasons.' He raised his finger to make his point. 'When I say that, the wrong reasons are the right reasons in this instance. It is intended to curse, hurt, and kill those it is used against, nothing less than pure evil.'

'Wow,' Annie said shaking her head. 'I never thought of it like that. I assumed it was because it was an 'old' language.'

'You must remember that the practitioners of the dark arts have been hunted and burned for possessing the knowledge. Those that hunted them were usually of low intelligence and only spoke English, therefore they couldn't decipher the text.' He turned the pages and read the headings on each one. 'Draconic evil, the Temple of Set, Typhon, Ahriman the Persian Devil and his Whore of Darkness. The Gnostic Yaldabaoth and the diabolic sorcery of Zoroastrian demonology are all in here.' He shivered and closed the book. 'This is an anthology of the most evil traditions known to mankind. The fact that society can dismiss its exponents as charlatans is testament to its power. It lays hidden, as do the people who can decipher it.' He put his hands into his pockets and looked Stirling square in the eye. 'This is not a book of spells as you see it. Dismiss it at your peril, Sergeant, because the woman who spent months preparing this house for the ceremony, killing vermin, coming and going unseen for months, is far more dangerous than you can imagine. To have a narrow mind at this juncture would be a mistake. She is incredibly powerful and incredibly evil, not a good combination from your perspective. There will be more victims.'

'We only have your opinion on that. If there was a woman here at all,' Stirling said pointedly. 'If there was, she is a lunatic and nothing more.'

'Then explain to me how she lured two strangers across the city to a specific address on a specific day.' He shrugged as he spoke. 'Not just any random day but a Satanic Sabbath. She subdued them both, slaughtered one and convinced the other to indulge in eating severed genitals, before disappearing into thin air and leaving him here to carry the blame for the murder. How did she do that, if she was a lunatic?' He wagged his finger again. Stirling flushed red. 'You cannot explain it because you don't understand it. There are dark forces at work, which you will not understand until you accept that they exist in the mind of your killer. Whether you believe or not is not important.'

'Pardon me for interrupting.' Kathy Brooks poked her head into the room. 'The footprints in the front room,' she said, looking at Annie. She held up her fingers. 'Three sets, two male, which match your victim and your suspect and one smaller narrower pair which I would say belonged to a female. I can't tell you that they were all made at the same time yet, but your suspect may be telling the truth that there was a woman here.'

'You need to keep this book somewhere secure, Inspector,' Arthur said, a little worried. 'She will be returning for it at some stage, probably after the third day of fasting has passed.'

'You think that she will come back here?' Annie asked incredulously. 'Despite the fact that we have found Bishop's body, and the place is teeming with police officers?'

'She needs that book. I would go so far to say that she lives for that book. It's more than her bible, much more.' He nodded, rubbing his chin. 'She did not think that you would find it. Indeed, why would you be looking for it at all?'

Annie nodded to Stirling. He begrudgingly picked up two large evidence bags from Kathy's kit trolley.

'I'll have it sent to secure evidence storage. It will look right at home next to the automatic weapons and class-A drug seizures.' He shook his head as he walked past Arthur and mumbled, 'I wonder if they have got a 'book of spells' shelf?'

ASHWORTH MENTAL HOSPITAL
23.15

'It is most irregular, Inspector,' a tired- looking doctor said, shaking his head. 'To be asked to perform this procedure at this time of night is bad enough but to turn up here for results is a bit much.'

'We have a warrant to inspect his stomach contents, which has been signed by a High Court Judge.' Annie handed him a piece of paper, which the doctor ignored. He pushed it towards a portly matron as if it was too hot to hold. 'Once we have the information we have asked for and we can see his contents, we want to interview him immediately.'

'The procedure should have been done by now, but the man is virtually catatonic.'

'Okay, we'll see what condition he's in once we know what was in his stomach,' Annie insisted. 'The contents of his stomach are vital to a murder investigation.'

'There really is no need to repeat yourself. I understand the importance of it,' the doctor said nervously. He turned quickly on his heels. 'It is a simple enough procedure to inspect the contents, however, I wasn't expecting to have to do it now!' He stormed off in the direction of the secure wards, his footsteps echoing down the corridor. 'Follow me, please,' he called behind him. Annie ran a couple of steps to catch up with him and then kept pace. She could hear Stirling ambling along behind them. 'He was confused when he arrived, but he had moments of being lucid. When we told him that we had to pump his stomach, he became hysterical. I had an emergency on another ward, so I left them to it. Do you know how many patients I oversee here at night?'

'No.'

'All of them, and most of them are delusional and violent,' he moaned. He blew air from his lungs in disgust as if Annie was solely responsible for the tight budgets. 'One consultant from six until six, to look after over two hundred men who have lost their minds.' He shrugged dramatically. 'That is why your request is a giant pain in the arse.'

'We appreciate your position, but this is a particularly nasty murder investigation with others possibly at risk,' Annie said, trying to keep her breathing level. He swiped his card through a security scanner and a set of double doors opened. The heady aroma of disinfectant met them, but beneath it, Annie could smell vomit and excrement. 'Is he sedated?'

The doctor seemed to ignore her question and came to a halt outside room 4. He looked inside and rapped on a glass porthole with his knuckles. There was a second's delay and then a male nurse appeared with a glass jar in his hand. His green fatigues were spattered with bodily fluid. He eyed the detectives with the same disdain as the doctor had showed towards them.

'Stomach contents and one very pissed off patient,' he handed the jar to the doctor and stared at Annie.

'Have you inspected it?'

'I didn't know what we were looking for, so I haven't looked properly.'

'What are you looking for, Inspector?' the doctor asked, inspecting the soupy liquid.

'Body parts.'

'Oh, I see the reason for the urgency.' Some larger meaty lumps nudged the glass. He frowned and twirled the jar. His eyes widened, and he tapped the glass with his middle finger. 'Oh Jesus,' he whispered and looked sternly at Annie. 'I think there is a penis in here.'

'That is what we're looking for,' Annie grimaced. 'We think that he ate his victim's genitals.'

The nurse sucked in his breath noisily, making a whistling sound. The doctor puffed his cheeks and shook his head as he inspected the contents.

'We're looking for the full set,' Stirling added gruffly. 'The meat and two veg.'

The medical men exchanged shocked glances but couldn't find the words they were looking for.

'I am pretty sure that we have the 'full set' in here,' the doctor said flatly.

'Bingo,' Stirling said gruffly. 'We're going to need the contents as evidence.'

'We need to speak to him,' Annie said.

The doctor was too taken aback to argue. He nodded to the nurse.

'Escort them, will you,' he sighed, looking at his pager. 'I'll have this examined thoroughly but we won't have the full results until tomorrow. I'm needed on another wing.'

He held up the jar once more and then turned and walked away.

'Just when you think that you have seen it all,' he said as he walked away. 'Nurse Walker will show you out when you're done.'

'I'm not sure what you'll get out of him, but I'll do my best to help. Follow me.'

The detectives followed the nurse through a series of dimly-lit corridors. Screams and manic laughter echoed from the walls. The nurse caught the expression on Annie's face.

'They don't sleep easily in here,' the nurse said.

'I'm not sure I would either,' Annie replied.

They reached the room, and the nurse swiped his card through the reader and opened the door. The name on the tab at the end of the metal cot said Jerry Bracknall. The young man was held down with thick leather straps, his wrists and ankles handcuffed to anchor points. He lifted his head as they entered the room. A sensor triggered the lights above his bed. He blinked his eyes and narrowed them, blinded by the light.

'You've got visitors, Jerry, although I don't suppose they've brought grapes.'

'I need a drink,' Jerry moaned. 'My throat is sore.' He looked to Annie for sympathy. 'They shoved a pipe down my throat,' he mumbled.

'We need you to tell us what happened to Barry Bishop first,' Annie said, walking to the bed. 'What do you remember?'

'The stench. It made me want to puke.' He closed his eyes and turned his head away. 'Then she came out of the shadows. She jumped on him like a mad woman.'

'Was this the naked woman?'

'Yes,' he smiled weakly. 'She was covered in writing all over her body.' He stopped smiling as he explained. His voice dropped to a whisper, as if someone might hear them. 'She was so strong. I've never seen anything like it. She picked him up like he was a child and carried him into the front room.'

'Can you describe her to me?'

'Pretty,' he garbled excitedly. His eyes brightened, and he seemed to wake up. 'Very pretty. Black hair. Long shiny black hair like silk,' he whispered. His eyes seemed to glaze as he remembered her. 'She's the most beautiful woman I've ever seen. Her eyes. So pretty.'

'Did she tell you her name?'

'Myra,' he smiled. 'She carried him like he was a child.'

'Did you know Myra before you went to the house?'

'No. I don't think so.' He looked away again.

'You don't think so?'

'I've never seen her before.'

'That's a lie, isn't it?'

'I can't remember.'

'Did you see her kill Barry Bishop?'

'Sort of.'

'You did, or you didn't.'

'I was there but I couldn't move.' He looked from the nurse to Annie and then to Stirling. 'It was like a dream.'

'So, you watched her kill him?'

'I think so. Unless it's all a nightmare?'

'Were you restrained?'

'Not physically, but I was mentally. I couldn't think. I couldn't speak. I couldn't move.'

'You couldn't move?'

'No. I was frozen to the spot.'

'At what point did you eat his genitals?' Stirling jumped straight in.

'No. I did not!' He fought against the restraints, arms and legs thrashing about. 'Don't you say that!' he shouted, his face darkening with anger. 'Don't you dare say that I did that!'

'Why not?'

'Because it's sick!'

'It is sick, but we found them in your stomach.'

'I couldn't have done something like that,' Jerry protested. 'I'm not like her. She was all lovey-dovey at firsts. I thought it was just a game but she's fucking nuts.'

Annie and Stirling exchanged glances.

'So, you were coerced into the murder?'

'I don't remember.' He calmed down instantly and looked confused. 'You found genitals in my stomach?' he asked, as quietly as a mouse would. His eyes seemed to roll back into his head.

'Is he drugged?'

'Not to that degree.' Nurse Walker shook his head and folded his arms. Stirling grabbed Bracknall's shoulder and shook him roughly.

'What, what,' he mumbled. 'Where am I?'

'Ashworth,' Stirling growled.

'Why am I here again?'

'Because you lured an innocent man to an empty house, slaughtered him and ate his tackle,' Stirling said flatly. 'Get used to being strapped down because you'll be in them for a very long time unless you start remembering what you did.' He leaned over the bed and glared at him.

His eyes focused again, and he tried to sit up.

'I can't tell you anything. She'll kill me.' He whispered.

'She can't get to you in here.'

'Oh, but she can.' His eyes darted nervously. 'She has followers everywhere.'

'You had better get used to lying in your own crap then, sunshine.' Stirling moved away. 'The way things stand, you're going to be charged with murder. We only have your word that there was a woman there. We'll be back in the morning to charge you.' He nodded to Annie and they walked towards the door. 'Case closed.'

'Wait, wait, wait,' Bracknall whispered. He swallowed hard. 'She told me that all I had to do was to get him to the house,' he whispered. 'She said that she would do the rest and all I had to do was watch and I would be initiated and could fuck her.' Jerry looked around, frightened someone would hear him. 'I was just trying to fuck her and then she got all weird on me. She lied to me. She drugged me, she must have. I was there but she made me do stuff that I didn't want to.' He looked at them, wide eyed. 'I just couldn't help myself. It was like I was watching from a dream. I had no control over my actions, I swear I didn't have any choice. She made me eat his bits and pieces, said that was my test. When I came around, I was covered in blood and the police were there.'

'How could she have drugged you?'

'I don't know.'

'Have you run toxicology?' Annie asked the nurse.

'We do it as part of the initial examination,' he nodded. 'I'll make a note on his charts to look for hypnotics and Rohypnol.'

Annie nodded and turned back to Bracknall. 'So, you did know her before?'

'Yes.' He closed his eyes as he spoke. 'I was messing about with swinger sites online and she found me. She befriended me and then it got a bit out of control.'

'Explain.'

'She was fit, and I've never been with a black girl,' he explained.

'She is black?'

'Yes, didn't I say?'

'No, you didn't.'

'Sorry, well she's black,' he shrugged. 'She told me that there were a group of them, all women and they wanted a male to join them for some occult fun.' He lowered his voice again. 'You know what I mean, like orgies and stuff. What would you do?' He smiled and looked at Stirling for male support. 'She said that her friend worked for an estate agent and all I had to do was to get her colleague to the property and I would be invited to their sessions. I could join their cult. I didn't think they took it seriously. I thought it was all about group sex.'

'Wait a minute,' Annie snapped. 'Back up a bit. What friend at an estate agent?'

'She wouldn't tell me her name but when I got to the office, there were two of them working there.'

'And Myra indicated that one of the women there was party to this?'

'So, Myra said.' He looked confused as he answered. 'I had some tea,' he mumbled and looked surprised as if something startling had occurred to him.

'What?'

'I had tea.' He tried to sit up, but the restraints snapped him back. 'I had two cups of tea. The fucking bitch must have spiked my tea!' he said excitedly. 'No wonder I was off my tits. They drugged my tea!'

'Who made the tea?'

'Carrie.' He grinned at the memory. 'Her name was Carrie.'

Stirling checked his notes and nodded his head. 'Carrie Drake.' He confirmed the name. 'She's on the list of employees.'

'Have we got an address?' Annie asked hopefully.

'I don't think so.' Stirling shook his head. There was no reason to look at her as a suspect. 'The office staff reported Bishop missing. We didn't need any addresses. I'll get someone on it now.' He looked at his watch and frowned. 'They'll be opening up at nine. Should we wait?'

'Yes,' Annie said. 'Let them think that Jerry here is taking the rap. We'll bring her in tomorrow. Get someone to put eyes on her tonight, just in case. We need to watch her and the house in case they go back for that book.'

'She set me up, didn't she?' Jerry Bracknall said excitedly. 'What a relief. They set me up good and proper.' He tried to sit up again. 'When can I get out of here?'

'I wouldn't get too excited just yet,' Stirling said gruffly. 'You went to that office with the intention of luring a man to an empty house, where someone was waiting for you. You may not have realised what was going to happen, but you were complicit in his death. Either way, you'll be locked up for a long time.'

'But it was just a laugh for me,' he whined. 'I just wanted to get her and her mates naked. I am innocent here!'

You're stupid at best, but innocent, no,' Annie shook her head.

'I was drugged.'

'We'll see when the tox reports come back.'

'I didn't know what I was doing.'

'You're an accomplished actor. That's for sure.'

'What?'

'A few hours ago, you were a jabbering wreck.'

'I was drugged and in shock,' he protested with his jaw hanging open. Something in his eyes told Annie that he was suddenly very frightened.

'The doctor described you as almost catatonic,' Stirling added.

'He has made a remarkable recovery,' the nurse commented sarcastically, his eyebrows raised.

'I am not convinced that you didn't know what was happening, Mr Bracknall.' Annie smiled thinly. 'Your story just doesn't ring true with me.' She turned and walked to the door. The nurse swiped his pass and it clicked open. 'We'll be back tomorrow sometime.'

09.00 QUICK MOVE UK Office

Carol Harris hadn't even taken her coat off when Carrie Drake burst through the office door with far more enthusiasm than the early hour required.

'Oh my God, I didn't sleep a wink,' she said dramatically, closing the door behind her. She noticed that there were more cars than usual parked outside and they all had people in them which was unusual. There was a twenty-minute limit on their street. Most people parked up and darted into whichever shop they were going to and then left before the wardens pounced. 'I could not get poor Barry out of my mind.' She rolled her eyes and walked towards her desk. 'I feel so guilty about being a complete bitch to him all the time. I didn't like him, that's the truth, but I wouldn't have wished him dead. Have you heard anything from the police?' She paused to take her coat off.

'No, nothing yet,' Carol lied. She couldn't tell Carrie that uniformed officers had knocked on her door at midnight asking questions and requesting her address. She avoided eye contact, as she was a terrible liar. Most of the time anyway. 'I wasn't sure if we should open up at all. It seems disrespectful to Barry, but business is business.'

'You can't afford to lose any potential customers, Carol,' Carrie said, checking her make-up in her compact mirror. 'This place has been like a graveyard for months.' She inhaled loudly and covered her mouth with her hand. 'Oh, I can't believe that I said that. How awful. I am such a bimbo sometimes. Fancy saying graveyard after poor old Barry was murdered.' She put her palms against her cheeks and shook her head. 'Oh well, shall we have a cup of tea?'

Carol was about to answer when a group of people approached the front door. Annie Jones walked in followed by Stirling and half a dozen others.

'Carol Harris?' Annie asked, showing her warrant card. Both employees stared at her. Carol noticed two more officers entering dressed in white paper jumpsuits.

'I'm Carol.'

'DI Annie Jones,' Annie said, studying both women. Carrie Drake looked very nervous. Her face had flushed red and she was clearly shaking. 'We need to ask you some questions about what happened yesterday.'

'Yes of course,' Carol said nervously. 'Can we make everyone a drink?'

'I'll go,' Carrie said. 'How many people are there?' She counted with her finger. 'I don't think we have enough cups.' She giggled nervously.

'We're fine,' Annie said, 'but you can show my detectives where you make tea, please?'

'Where we make the tea?' she frowned and looked to her boss for an explanation. Carol shrugged and grimaced.

'Yes,' Annie nodded and smiled. 'Please show Sergeant Stirling where you make the tea. We have a warrant, Carol, nothing to worry about, just procedure.' Carrie nodded open mouthed and looked worried. She looked at her employer for permission and Carol nodded yes.

'This way,' she mumbled. 'The kitchen is in the back.' Her shoulders slumped as she led the way.

'I'm sorry,' Carol said. 'She's a little bit dizzy sometimes but she's very good at selling houses.'

'Do you know any of her friends?' Annie got straight to the point. She wanted to catch them off guard. Carol's eyes flickered. She was searching for an answer.

'Erm, not really. We don't socialise outside of work,' Carol frowned. 'Except at Christmas of course.'

'Do any of her friends call her?'

'I'm not a fan of them using their mobiles in my time.'

'She must talk about what she has done over the weekend.' Annie smiled disarmingly. 'You know how we girls like to gossip.'

'Well, she does like to talk a lot,' Carol laughed nervously.

'Any names come up regularly?'

'Not that I can recall.' She looked away as she spoke. 'She says, 'me and the girls did this or me and the girls did that,' they're always up to something.'

'Have you heard the name Myra?'

'No.'

'Are any of her girlfriends black?'

'Gosh,' Carol grimaced. 'Erm, I really wouldn't know that. I wouldn't think to ask her.'

'Is this her desk?' Annie said, walking to where her coat was slung on the back of a chair. Carol nodded that it was. 'Had you ever seen Jerry Bracknall before yesterday?'

'No, never.' She shook her head vehemently. A little too vehemently for Annie. Something wasn't right at Quick Move. 'Have you charged him yet?'

Annie thought for a moment. Maybe Carol Harris was just shocked. 'Not yet. He has to be assessed mentally first.'

'Of course. He must be a bloody nutter, anyway,' Carol tutted. 'He seemed so normal. You can't tell, can you?'

'No, you can't.'

'I was going to go there.' She choked on her words. A sob escaped her lips. 'I asked Barry to go at the last minute. I feel so guilty.'

'You shouldn't,' Annie calmed her. She glanced through the doorway into the back corridor. There was no sign of Carrie Drake. 'Did Carrie act oddly yesterday when Bracknall came into the office?' Annie saw the flicker in her eyes again.

'No more than usual.' Carol smiled coyly, wiping a tear away. She took a deep breath and composed herself. 'She comes alive when handsome men walk in. It's as if she has an 'on' switch.'

'Did she seem familiar with him?'

'She is familiar with them all.' Carol tutted and shook her head. 'Inspector, is there something that I should know about? Why are you asking all these questions about Carrie?'

'Because Barry Bishop wasn't at that house by chance.' Annie studied her reaction. 'We think that he was lured to that address by his killer.'

'How on earth could that be?' Carol frowned, shocked. 'Jerry Bracknall was a random customer looking for a flat.' She shook her head in disbelief. 'It was Barry that mentioned number 44 in the first place. I'm sure it was.'

'Bracknall told us that he didn't come here by accident,' Annie explained. 'He was told to come here.' She walked to the advertising boards and glanced at them. 'Would Barry have suggested taking clients to that property as the norm?'

'Only if they couldn't afford anything else that we had.'

'Did Bracknall indicate that he had limited funds?'

'Yes.'

'Guv,' Stirling called from the doorway which led into the office backups. 'You need to see this.' Annie smiled at Carol in apology and walked across the office. The doorway led to a narrow corridor. On one side was a small toilet and the kitchenette was on the other. Carrie Drake looked lost, as forensic officers searched the cupboards and a small fridge. One of them held up a bottle of milk as she entered.

'There is Rohypnol in the milk, Guv.'

'Carrie?' Annie turned to the baffled woman. 'Did Myra tell you to drug Jerry Bracknall?' Carrie began to cry. Tears rolled from her eyes, and she wiped them away with her sleeves. 'He told me that you made him two cups of tea yesterday before they left for Brick Street. Did you drug him?'

'I want a solicitor,' Carrie stammered. 'I have absolutely no fucking idea what you're talking about and I'm not saying another thing until I've spoken to my brief.' She folded her arms stubbornly. 'I didn't poison anybody, that's bullshit!'

'We will have to arrest you, Carrie.' Annie cocked her head and looked into her eyes. 'Why don't you tell us what happened off your own back, otherwise it will go against you.' Carrie pouted and shook her head negatively. 'Okay, have it your way.' She gestured to Stirling. 'Arrest her for conspiracy to commit murder. That will do for a start.'

'What?' Carrie shouted. 'Are you mad?'

'You had your chance,' Annie said grimly. 'Take her to the station and get her a solicitor. I want a warrant to search her address and we'll take it from there.' Annie left her with a confused expression and steam blowing from her ears as she was read her rights. She looked confused and very angry, but she didn't look like a murderer, and she didn't look guilty either.

'Search their desks,' Annie instructed two detectives. 'Do Barry Bishop's first and then do Carrie's.' She wandered back into the main office. As Carrie was led away, Annie watched Carol Harris looking on in disbelief and talking on the telephone. She appeared to be very distressed, which under the circumstances wasn't too unusual. When she came off the phone, Annie approached her. 'We found Rohypnol in the milk.'

'Fucking hell,' Carol hissed. 'I don't believe this.' She looked as the detectives searched the desks. 'That was my mother on the telephone. She's worried about me. The entire family is in shock. She babysits my daughter when the schools are off.'

'I see,' Annie said. 'It will be a very difficult time for you, I'm sure. We'll be as quick as we can and then we'll leave you to run your business in peace.' Annie frowned. 'Will you get agency staff in to replace them for now?'

'I have no idea.' Carol had to dig deep to stay calm and not implode into a quivering heap. Business was the last thing on her mind.

'I need to get back to the station,' Annie grimaced. 'I am sorry for disrupting things, but I am sure you understand that we have a job to do. I'll be in touch.'

An hour later, the remaining detectives left without saying a word to her. Carol felt alone but relieved that her office had returned to something like normal. She picked up her mobile and walked to the front window. The officers drove by and gave her a last glance. One of them nodded and smiled thinly. If it was a thank you and goodbye, then so be it. She was glad to see the back of them. Carol dialled and waited.

'They've gone,' she said, smiling. 'I was so nervous.'

'What happened?'

'They asked a lot of questions about Carrie and then arrested her.'

'Why would they arrest Carrie?'

'They found Rohypnol in the fridge,' Carol explained. 'It was in the milk.'

'I told you to make sure that the milk was thrown out.'

'Yes, but you didn't tell me there was something in it!' Carol protested. 'What if someone else had drunk it?'

'They didn't. You were told to throw it out.'

'I just forgot,' Carol said apologetically. 'Please don't be mad. Yesterday was such a blur. I was going to throw it this morning, but they came in seconds after me. I just didn't have time.'

'That is a mistake.'

'I am sorry.'

'I want you and Sophie to stay with me at Christmas,' Myra said sternly. It wasn't a request. 'It will keep you out of the spotlight while things settle down.'

'Sophie stays with mum at Christmas.' Carol sounded unsure. Scared even. 'They take her to the caravan at Towyn.'

'You will both stay here,' Myra snapped. 'I will expect you after work tonight. Do not tell anyone where you are going.'

'Okay.' Carol half smiled. 'I love you. See you later.' She waited for a response in kind but all she heard was static.

TWO DAYS LATER

'Thanks for coming in, Arthur,' Annie said as she walked into her office. He stood and smiled at her but there was concern in his eyes. His navy-blue suit was tight around the shoulders. 'I am in dire need of some help.'

'I have been keeping up with the newspapers, but they don't say much,' he said

with a sigh. 'I hoped that it wasn't as I predicted.'

'I really hope that you're wrong, but things have taken a turn for the worse,' Annie said shaking her head. 'We have arrested Jerry Bracknall, but he claims to have been drugged before they left the estate agents. We found Rohypnol in the office kitchen and arrested a woman who made him two cups of tea. Bracknall claims that he was set up. He says that he went along with it on the promise of sex with a group of women who belonged to a coven.'

'That is how these people work,' Arthur agreed. 'Sex in return for an act of wrongdoing is a powerful reward.'

'The woman we arrested for drugging him isn't talking,' Annie explained. 'She denied any knowledge of anything, and we don't have any evidence to prove it was her. However, her employer, Carol Harris, has gone missing.'

'Missing?'

'Carol Harris took her daughter to visit a friend, but we haven't heard from her since and I remember you warning us about a certain ceremony which involved a woman and younger girl, I just can't remember its name, but a mother and daughter fits the bill.'

'The Da Muer Ritual, which is the rape, torture and sacrifice of a woman and young girl, preferably related and ideally mother and daughter.' His face darkened. 'You fear that Carol Harris and her daughter were taken as offerings?'

'You said that they often source their victims from within the group?'

'Yes.' Arthur smiled thinly. 'You have impressed me with your memory, Inspector. Most people would regard it as gobbledegook.'

'Normally, I would too, but we don't have any answers so I'm open minded for now.'

'Indeed.' He smiled. 'They source from within because there is a level of trust. Kidnapping a mother and daughter off the street would be difficult, if not impossible, but if the mother is coerced into their circle, then they could be persuaded to bring their children with them. Disposing of remnants is simple enough. Especially when most of the body would be consumed during ritual.' He paused to think for a second. 'I did some research on that book, Inspector, and I think it is known in occult circles as The Book of Abominations, which has been missing for centuries. Some of the ceremonies within it encourage a virtual feeding frenzy, which can last for days. There would not be much left of the victims.'

'We think that it is too much of a coincidence that Carol Harris and her daughter have vanished. There has been no movement on her phone or her bank account,' Annie explained. 'We're trying to track down the friend who she visited but we've drawn a blank. The last call that she made was to a prepaid cell, which was never used again. We fear the worst I'm afraid.'

Arthur Cross sat back in his chair and cradled his chin between his finger and thumb. He looked deep in thought and his solid frame looked slightly deflated by the news.

'I'm not sure how I can help you, Inspector. Did you have some specific questions for me?'

'I am clutching at straws, Arthur,' Annie shrugged. 'Who would do this? Tell me who I am looking for.' She put her palms flat on the desk. 'Where can I look for them?'

'I have been giving it a lot of thought and I think I know where you should look,' Arthur said quietly. His eyes burned into her head as if reading her mind. 'But you must answer me a question first.'

Annie shuffled uncomfortably in her seat. 'Ask away.'

'Where is the book?'

'Why would you ask that?' she blushed. She leaned forward and returned his searching gaze. Her fingers tapped nervously on the desk.

'Where is it?' He looked into her eyes and tilted his head slightly. 'I need you to tell me where that book is.'

'Why, Arthur?' she snapped. His persistence had her on the back foot. 'Why is it so important?'

'Because I know it is being used.'

'How?'

'You wouldn't understand.' Arthur stood up and walked to the window. A lone magpie landed on the ledge below him. 'One for sorrow,' he said. He looked back at Annie and sighed.

'Try me.' Annie sat back. She crossed her legs and waited for him to answer. 'Like I said earlier, I have an open mind for now.'

'There has been a paradigm shift in the balance of things, Inspector.' He exhaled and searched for the right words. He touched the jagged scars on his head unconsciously. 'The scales are tipped strongly in favour of the left-hand path. Whoever is using that book knows its power and they're using it to create chaos. Where is it, before it is too late?'

'We don't know,' Annie admitted. She wasn't surprised that he knew it was missing but the fact that he did know sent her sense of reality reeling. 'We didn't know until yesterday, but it never arrived at the evidence lock-up.'

'My God.' He closed his eyes and sighed into his hands. 'Did it leave that house?'

'What?'

'This is vital,' he said slowly. 'Did it leave that house?'

'We don't know for sure,' she sighed. 'Sergeant Stirling bagged it and tagged it to be taken by the evidence teams, but it was never logged in. The chances are that it didn't reach the CSI vehicle at all.'

'I think it is right under your nose, Inspector, and so is Carol Harris.'

'Please don't be cryptic with me, Arthur,' Annie said shaking her head. 'The entire case is nothing but a mind-fuck from beginning to end. If you have a theory, please share it with me.'

'Jerry Bracknall said that your killer arrived from under the stairs, right?'

'Yes, Jerry Bracknall said that, but he was complicit. I can't believe his version of events.'

'Whoever prepared that house came and went for months without being seen,' he shrugged. 'How could that book have been taken from under the noses of the CSI officers, unless the thief had access to the property?' He paused for a moment. 'I think that they're next door. I am sure that the adjoining neighbours have been canvassed by your officers but unless using the Dark Arts can suddenly render one invisible, they must be able to get into that house at will.'

'You think someone has access to number 44 via a neighbouring property?'

'How else can they gain entry without being seen? She needs that book, I told you that, and she needs to be above contaminated ground yet remain unseen.' He wagged his finger. 'One or more of the neighbours is one of them. They're shielding them.'

Annie bit her bottom lip and thought about what he had said. She had a million questions to ask but they were relevant. His theory was credible, and it would explain a lot of conundrums surrounding the case.

'I think that you could be right,' she said, picking up her phone. 'I'll have both properties raided today. Fingers crossed that Carol Harris and her daughter are still alive.'

'The ceremony will not be performed until tomorrow,' he reassured her. 'One more thing, Inspector.' Arthur held up his hand to stop her.

'What?'

'The book.' He lowered his voice and leaned forward. 'We cannot allow it to fall into their hands again. Not ever.' He tensed his jaw; the veins in his temple pulsed quickly. 'I cannot explain the evil which follows that book, but you can research it in your own time. Google 'the abomination of desolation.' It will frighten you.' He nodded. 'Give the book to me for safe keeping. I have the skills to keep them from it.'

Annie wasn't sure why she had faith in his words, but she did. She nodded and stood up offering her hand. Arthur shook it and relaxed a little.

'If you're right, I'll make sure that you take possession of it for research purposes. You're deciphering it for us to see if it has any relevance to the case, okay?' Arthur smiled thinly and held her grip firmly. Keeping that book from them would be perilous, but he had no choice, and he couldn't trust anyone else with it. Its power was insidious; it tainted the morally pure and poisoned all it touched. Even the other occult librarians couldn't know of its existence.

44 BRICK STREET

The air in the cellar was barely breathable. The animal carcasses had been removed, but the putrid odour of their maggot-strewn, rotting flesh clung to the walls, the plaster and the timbers. Annie Jones crouched in her position waiting for the Forced Entry Teams to strike the houses on either side of 44. A detailed search of the cellar had revealed secret panels behind brick tiles, which had been aged to make them blend invisibly into the wall. The hatches were on either side leading into both adjoining properties. Surveillance officers had noted that no one appeared to leave the houses after dark.

Mary South in 42, worked for a small bank, paid her taxes and had no convictions. Helen Walters in 46, was registered disabled. She claimed the minimum benefits allowed and had no family listed as carers. Inconspicuous people or a front for a murderous cult? They were about to find out. Annie checked her body armour and clicked the comms unit to signal that they were in position.

'Green light, go, go, go.'

There was a series of dull vibrations and dust was sprinkled from the timbers above her. She heard muffled shouts and the sound of boots stomping on the floorboards upstairs. A wave of her hand signalled the cellar teams to move. They hammered through the brick panelling in seconds. The sound of splintering wood and cracking tiles filled the air, joined quickly by the voices of the first officers through the hatches.

'Armed police!' echoed through the confined space. 'Clear!'

'Clear already?'

Annie mumbled to herself. She walked across the cellar and peered into the gloom beneath 42. Torchlight illuminated it. The armed officers searched the area looking for other secret panels. There was an altar draped with a goat skin, the four-horned skull still attached. Thick church candles stood unlit; pentangles and other symbols that she didn't recognise were painted on the walls. The 'Sigil of Baphomet' was marked out on the floor.

'Where are the stairs?' she asked, confused.

'There are none, Guv. The access into here is via number 44's cellar.'

'We've found something here!' A call came from beneath 46. Annie turned and crossed the cellar. She looked into a similar space and although there was no altar, the walls were covered in occult script and symbols. It was a dry- lined cellar with no obvious staircase to access the upper floors. 'Over here, Guv.'

A beam of light illuminated two grimy tear-streaked faces; their eyes looked frightened and animal like. They were crammed into a cage, which Annie guessed was designed for transporting a large dog. She recognised their features. Carol Harris had obviously lost weight. Her cheekbones protruded, and her eyes were sunken with deep black circles beneath them.

'Get them out of there,' she said, looking at the ceiling above them. There was a hatch in the far corner. 'Clever.' She nodded towards the hinges. 'Undetectable from inside the house. We wouldn't even know that there was a cellar beneath either house.'

There was a muffled scream from above and the sound of raised voices. Footsteps clattered across the floorboards. Three shots echoed off the walls, bang, bang, bang.

'Armed police!' drifted down to them followed by another three shots and high-pitched screams. Then there was a whooshing sound and louder screams, followed by the frantic sound of multiple pairs of feet running towards the front of the buildings. She felt searing heat from above and there was a hiss as the cellar air was sucked upwards.

'Get out now!' an officer shouted. 'Upstairs must be on fire.'

'Get them out of that cage!' Annie ordered. Two shots retorted in the cellar, the noise ear-splitting in the confined space. The padlock clattered across the floor. The cage door was ripped open, and Carol Harris was dragged out. An officer picked her up in his arms and sprinted for the hatch. Another took her from him and ran for the stairs. Her daughter was carried through a second later.

'Move, Guv!' Annie felt herself guided to the stairs; her feet hardly touched the ground, as she was carried forward by bigger, stronger male officers.

'Wait!' she shouted.

'What is it, Guv?'

'Was there a book on that altar?'

'No, nothing but the goatskin and some candles.' The officer held her elbow to stop her from losing her balance. Thick black smoke poured through the cracks between the rafters. She could hear the crackling and spitting of ferocious flames devouring dry wood. 'We need to move, Guv!'

'The fireplace!' she shouted and ran up the stairs. 'Follow me.' She turned to him as she took the steps three at a time. She burst into the hallway and through the open front door she caught sight of smoke billowing along the street. Annie ran through the living room into the smaller room at the rear of the house. The demonic fireplace dominated the room. She heard the officer stumbling behind her.

'Help me drag this,' she shouted. She knelt and gripped the hearth. The officer followed suit on the opposite side. 'Okay, ready?'

'Yes, Guv.'

'Pull!' She heaved as hard as she could. The slate seemed to tingle with energy. She closed her eyes and gritted her teeth, but the slab wouldn't budge. 'Come on, heave!'

'It's too heavy, Guv,' the officer gasped. Smoke made his exertion difficult.

'Move out of the way, quickly,' Stirling's voice boomed. The house was filling with thick black smoke. Acrid fumes stung their eyes and Annie felt her lungs beginning to burn. Stirling shoved the uniformed officer towards the door.

'Get out!' He gripped the hearth with his huge hands and pulled. The slate groaned against the floorboards and then moved to reveal the hidden pit. The skin-bound book had been replaced beneath the fireplace by someone. 'Grab it and get out, Guv!'

Annie reached inside and gripped the book. The covering of skin seemed to move beneath her fingers. She could swear that she could feel it pulsing, as if blood still throbbed through the veins. The sensation of being suffocated by a million flies returned. Images of maggots wriggling through puddles of congealing blood flashed in her brain. 'Move, Guv, do it now!'

Annie blinked and ran towards the front door, the book safely tucked beneath her arm. She cleared the front door and felt smoke spewing from her lungs. The crackling of flames had turned to a roar. The intensity of the heat forced her to keep running until she reached the safety of the line of emergency vehicles. She turned and looked at the terraced houses and for the first time realised the scale of the devastation. Flames poured from every window of number 42 and the entire upper storey of 46 was a raging inferno. The damaged roof of 44 was ablaze, the three fires desperately reaching out to each other, trying to become one. The fire brigade aimed three hoses into the conflagration and steam hissed skyward.

'Jesus Christ!' Annie wheezed. She looked around for arrested suspects. 'Tell me that we arrested them.' Stirling collapsed in a panting heap beside her. 'Did we make any arrests?'

'They had the entire place rigged to burn, Guv.' He shook his head. 'It was as if they knew that we were coming.' He coughed and spat on the road. 'As soon as we entered, they set fire to the houses and then themselves. They're all in there.' As if on cue, a figure appeared at the upstairs window of number 46. The entire body was engulfed by flame. She raised her arms up to the side and made the shape of the cross before tumbling from the window. The burning figure somersaulted in mid-air before becoming impaled on the spiked railings, which separated the houses from the pavement. It writhed and twitched for a long time before it became still. Annie heard a throaty gurgle which turned into a laugh. She looked around, shocked that anyone could find such a sight amusing, but there was nothing but revulsion on the faces around her.

She heard it again but this time she felt the book twitch. The gurgling laughter seemed to come from within.

4 Months Later
The Occult Librarian

HE DIDN'T THINK HE would be able to sleep, even though his eyes were sore and his body was exhausted. As he poured himself another scotch, he heard the clock chime. It was the witching hour and cold fingers of fear toyed with his mind sending a shiver up his spine. The living room window exploded in a shower of glass; lethal shards sent in every direction. They had come for the book.

He had kept the 'Book of Abominations' a secret for four months. It was like looking after a lump of irradiated uranium; it had infinite value but being near it for an extended period had damaging, if not lethal effects, on mere mortals. Arthur Cross had kept it hidden in a vault beneath his basement flat, opening it only for short periods to study its vile secrets. He could not allow them to retake it. The 'Abomination of Desolation' was clearly described in the evil bible. It was the beginning of the end of days. Several of the gospels warned of the power of the Abominations. He didn't know where the book had been for two thousand years, or how the dark ones had come across it, but he couldn't let it happen again.

He heard the security bars which protected the window being rattled by the would-be intruder. The security glass had failed but the rusty iron bars would outlive them all. Arthur ran to the gun cabinet and took the key from his silver necklace. He opened it and selected the Spanish Larona.

Breaking the gun, he loaded both barrels and altered the choke to maximise the width of the shot. It would make the killing zone greater when it was discharged. He walked towards the front door and sat in the armchair which faced it, pointing the shotgun at the latch. He listened intently. Tiny scratching sounds reached him; metal scraping against metal. He could hear a pick in one of the four locks. They had sent a buffoon. Not only had he announced his arrival by breaking the window, but he was also blatantly trying to pick his way into the home of a Librarian. Arthur walked to the door swiftly and quietly. He slid the barrels through the letter box and squeezed the trigger twice. The gun kicked and roared. He listened to the mewing, whimpering sound outside, reloaded the gun and unlocked the front door.

A badly-wounded youth lay curled in the foetal position on the bottom step; his intestines hung from his tracksuit, and they glistened in the moonlight. Blood ran from his mouth, dark blood from deep inside the guts, almost black in the gloom of the stairwell.

'Who sent you, you fool?' Arthur knelt next to him. He was late teens at best, probably lured with the promise of money and drugs. His lips moved silently, and his eyes rolled into his head. A garbled rasp came from his throat and then the death rattle followed.

''Hello.' A voice startled him. It came from the stairwell, its owner hidden in the gloom. 'You must be Arthur,' the voice said. The woman walked down three steps into view. The moonlight seemed to glint in her black eyes and her black skin had a matt sheen to it. 'I've come to collect my book,' Myra said smiling. Arthur felt the evil oozing from her. Her eyes were hypnotising, almost disabling.

'You can't enter this place,' he warned her. 'The lines are drawn at this doorway.'

'Your power is weakening, Librarian.' She smiled seductively. He could see how her followers succumbed to her will. She was hypnotisingly beautiful. 'The book is draining your energy, sucking the life from you. You could give me the book and I will be gone. Fetch it and be rid of it,' she smiled.

She was stunningly beautiful, no doubt about it and he wanted to do what she asked.

'It's a burden that will kill you eventually. It will sap the life from you a little at a time until there's nothing left but a shell.'

'Go to hell.' He broke her gaze, raised the shotgun, and fired. She took the force of the shot full in the face. The maelstrom of hot lead ripped the flesh from her left cheek and shattered her lower jaw, revealing her teeth and inner ear. She howled like a banshee and raised her hands. Arthur felt a thump in his chest as if he had been hit by a sledgehammer. The force of the blow knocked him back against the wall, cracking his head with enough of an impact to stun him. He felt consciousness slipping. Darkness descended but as he stared at it, the stairwell was darker still. It was as if ink had filled the space. The faces of the damned swirled at the edges, writhing in agony, screaming in pain. They were desperate to reach him, to drag him into the blackness, but they couldn't cross the line. Arthur's eyes flickered and then closed, his brain shut down by the force of the concussion.

THE SUN WAS SHINING when he awoke. He lifted his head, and a bolt of pain warned him not to move too quickly. The shotgun was next to him, the front door wide open. Myra, or whoever she really was, was gone. As was her minion. Their blood had turned black, appearing more like lichen than anything from a human. Arthur shook the shadows from his mind and pushed himself up. He stepped towards the doorway and felt a chill as he neared it. Her presence lingered. Despite the sunlight which filtered into the stairwell, her evil left its echo. Arthur slammed the door and locked it as if the wood could prevent the demons from entering. It wasn't the wood which had stopped her but good energy. Good magik. She couldn't cross the line of salt and energy. Of course, it couldn't last forever but it made him feel safer for now. She was right, his power was weakening. The Book of Abominations was feeding on his energy. She would be back unless he could find her first. Arthur needed help and he had heard about another man who hunted the Niners. He needed to find him, and he needed to find him quickly.

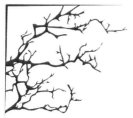

Chapter 1

Do you believe in ghosts?

It's a question we have all been asked before, right? I bet you have answered both yes and no at times. How many times have you changed your mind in your lifetime? I have chopped and changed a hundred times and probably lied on a few occasions too, especially as a young man. I think young men in their testosterone-fuelled teens and twenties are less likely to admit that they do believe, as if it's a weakness to be scared by anything. I once heard a macho remark which stayed with me.

'I'm not scared of ghosts. If a ghost ever came near me, I would punch it in the face. ...'

Okay, the guy was an idiot but there are several fundamental issues with the above statement. The first is to assume ghosts exist and are physical forms that can be punched, which is ridiculous. I have read many ghost hunters' reports but never read anything about a ghostly apparition being so close that it can be punched, therefore I am sure it hasn't happened. I also think that assuming ghosts exist and are here to harm us is a contradiction of our physical and mental boundaries; they are either here in physical form or they're not. If they are ethereal, they can't harm us.

Having researched the paranormal for years, there are too many stories and unexplained incidents to refute that paranormal energy doesn't exist, yet we have no absolute proof that can be used to silence the doubters. In the year 2023, with the technology available to us, if the dead could communicate with the living, wouldn't we know? It would be a brave person to stand up and say categorically that we can communicate with the dead because we would say, prove it. But can the dead still influence the living?

Recently, a friend of mine had a dream that her father (who has passed away) asked her where her nephew was and he sounded concerned about him. The dream disturbed her a little, but she didn't give it much thought. Her sister called at the house unexpectedly the next day and while they made a cup of tea and chatted, her nephew called her sister, which he rarely did (he worked away). He told his mum that he was struggling with his mental health and was feeling suicidal. Coincidence or something else, or can the dead influence the living?

Obviously, there are some sensitives amongst us who say they do communicate with the dead. Many make a living from it but once again, we're challenged by the lack of cold hard factual-based proof. I can't give you any answers, but I can share my experience and tell you what I think. We're all entitled to an opinion, whichever side of the fence you're on.

I think that energy and genetics are too powerful to die. Genetics pass from generation to generation for millenniums and are something we cannot deny. How do salmon know where they were spawned and return there as adults to spawn themselves? How do birds know where to fly to in the winter when it turns cold? Turtles return to the beach where they were hatched decades before to lay their own eggs; how do they know where it is?

We call it instinct, passed from generation to generation, unconscious learned behaviour. The DNA of each living thing passes on to the next generation. Energy and genetics are carried through time for millions of years.

Energy.

The universe is energy, light, heat, sound, forever shifting and changing shape and form. But we can't see it. Take a magnet for example. We can see it attracting other metal and repelling objects, but we can't see the energy which is causing the physical movement.

We all have energy, we understand it, we are marvelled by it, we know it is there, but we can't physically see it. Many years ago, I went to work on a house on a new estate near Southport. I was chatting to the lady who owned it and she told me that no birds flew into the gardens on the estate, something most of the residents were aware of. Some of the residents investigated the history of the site and discovered that for many years, it had been a slaughterhouse for chickens, turkeys and other fowl, so was that the reason birds avoided it?

The same phenomenon has been recorded many times at the site of mass death and slaughter. What does that prove? Animals can sense where death occurred many years after it's happened. They can see something we can't.

If you do believe in ghosts, you're not alone; if you don't, you're not alone either. Religions, tribes, sects, different cultures all around the planet believe in spirits that survive death to live in another realm. Isn't that the essence of religion? The Holy Ghost. The Holy Spirit. The Holy Ghost is mentioned 385 times in the New Testament bible, so if Jesus can be a ghost...there must be others?

Ghosts are part of our DNA because of religion. Be good in life and you don't actually die; you live forever, somewhere else that's really nice. Or if you are bad, you still get to live forever, somewhere really shit. It's enough to bend your mind out of shape. Religion is a subject for another day but for those who believe in a God, the afterlife is guaranteed, one way or the other.

Ghosts are among the most widely believed of all paranormal phenomenon: we're fascinated by it. Millions of people are interested in ghosts, and thousands read ghost stories every day. How many films have you seen with ghosts, spooks, spirits and possessions in the plotline?

There are literally hundreds out there, I bet but it's more than mere entertainment. The idea that the dead remain with us in spirit is an ancient one, appearing in countless stories. It has spawned legends and folklore from the beginning of time. Belief in ghosts is part of other related paranormal beliefs, such as near-death experience, life after death, and actual communication with the dead. This belief offers many people comfort and I get that. People like the thought that their loved ones are still here, looking out for us. Isn't that the principle of Christianity, that a benevolent spirit is constantly watching and protecting?

My problem with this is that some people want to communicate with the dead for the wrong reasons. If people believe in benevolent spirits, such as God, then we have to consider that there are malevolent spirits too. Evil people seek to harness these dark forces for evil reasons. Not everyone who has passed over was a good person, right?

Humans have tried to communicate with spirits throughout the ages. In Victorian England, for example, it was fashionable for the upper-class ladies to hold séances in their parlours after tea and cakes with their friends. Ouija boards and tarot cards were common for decades, like a Monopoly game that everyone can play but with dead people. Parlour games that scare the pants off you in the safety of your own home.

There have been ghost-hunting clubs around for years. Universities such as Cambridge and Oxford had societies to investigate ghosts and hauntings in the 1800s. In 1882, one of the most prominent organisations, the Society for Psychical Research, was established, essentially ghost hunters.

People have been taking ghosts seriously for a long time. In America during the late 1800s, many psychic mediums claimed to speak to the dead—but were later exposed as frauds by sceptical investigators such as Barry Houdini. There are many contradictions inherent in ideas about ghosts. For example, are ghosts physical, material beings or not? Either they can move through solid objects without disturbing them, like floating through a wall, which makes them vapour-like, or they can slam doors shut and throw objects across the room. According to logic and the laws of physics, it's one or the other. But do the laws of physics as we understand them apply?

It wasn't until recently that I became seriously interested in ghost hunting. My interest was piqued by Syfy series, Ghost Hunters, which aired over 200 episodes and found no solid evidence of the existence of ghosts. The premise of the show was that anyone can look for ghosts. Me included. You don't need to be a scientist or have any training in paranormal investigation. All you need is time, a potentially-haunted place, and maybe a few EMF gadgets from an electronics store. Anything unexplained could be deemed as evidence of a ghost and that cloudy criteria is part of the reason why myths about the afterlife are so prevalent. What would you accept as evidence of a ghost?

The difficulty in scientifically evaluating the evidence of ghosts is immense. There are a myriad of phenomena which are attributed to ghostly activity, from a door closing on its own, to missing items or items being moved, a cold spot in a hallway, to an actual vision of a dead relative. Millions of people report something uncanny happening to them, but most are not sure that they had encountered a ghost, and many remain uncertain that such phenomena is possible, despite their experience.

Many of the people on record, report experiencing something uncanny, something inexplicable, extraordinary, mysterious, or eerie but can't explain it. Sound familiar?

Personal experience is one thing, but scientific evidence is another matter. Part of the difficulty in investigating ghosts is that there is not one universally agreed upon definition of what a ghost is. Some believe that they are spirits of the dead who for whatever reason get lost on their way to the other side. Others claim that ghosts are instead telepathic entities projected into the world from our minds, while other say they might be recordings of something that happened, replayed by our brain. The simple answer is, we don't know.

When considering the existence of ghosts, there are some simple questions to ask yourself.

1. If ghosts are human souls, why do they appear clothed and with inanimate objects like clothes, hats, canes, and so on—not to mention reports of ghost ships, trains, cars?

2. If ghosts are the spirits of those whose deaths were unavenged, why are there unsolved murders? Surely the ghosts would simply communicate with psychic mediums, and identify their killers for the police?

The ghost hunters I have met use many creative methods to detect the presence of the dead, often including psychics, but how can we assume they're all legitimate? Many of them claim to use a purely scientific approach by using high-tech scientific equipment, including electromagnetic field detectors, infrared cameras and microphones. Yet none of this equipment has ever been proven to actually detect ghosts. Not ever.

Okay, I'm arguing the facts as I see them, yet Albert Einstein suggested a scientific basis for the reality of ghosts, based on the First Law of Thermodynamics which goes back to my earlier point.

Energy.

Energy is energy and can change form but cannot be destroyed. Einstein said that if energy cannot be created or destroyed but can only change form, what happens to our body's energy when we die? Could that energy be manifested as a different form of energy, good and evil? Let me continue to tell the story of 44 Brick Street and then make your mind up.

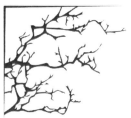

Chapter 2

T he story begins with a Facebook contact many months before and the communication that it led to. To cut a long story short, I was invited to an occult bookstore in Liverpool to look at a collection of historical documents, books and scripts collected over decades by several well-respected paranormal investigators. They had spent years investigating hauntings in the Old Swan area of Liverpool. The reports of strange goings on date back to the plague in 1347, until current day and were compiled into one study by an expert on all things weird and wonderful, the shop owner, Arthur Cross. I had heard of the bookshop before, and it was mentioned to me online by a woman called Galia Manx. Galia made a living by consulting online.

Galia presented herself as a very articulate professional. She clearly loved what she was doing. She told me that she had researched the documented sightings and hauntings, and her enthusiasm was admirable. Galia talked about the hauntings with a passion that I have never encountered before. Her passion was almost an obsession, and her enthusiasm was infectious. The information she gathered is so detailed and consistent over centuries, it must be taken seriously.

The oldest writings were by a Franciscan monk called Ganzalo who arrived on a ship from Madrid around the same time as the plague. His diaries document how hard Liverpool was hit by the disease as a city, and depict the following chaos, death and devastation it created. His journals and scrolls document the beginning of an unexplainable chain of events, which continues to present day, backed up by countless other articles written by dozens of journalists, historians and investigators.

It all adds up to some startling events that are hard to decipher and explain but the question is, are they all true?

Lies, legends and hoaxes are legion and can last forever but the details waver and there are always holes in the fiction. Merlin the wizard, King Arthur, and the knights of the round table are so entrenched in our psyche, people twist the facts to fit the fiction, yet no one can categorically say where they lived and died. People guess that Tintagel is the castle where Arthur reigned but there is no proof. St George, the patron saint of England, slayed a dragon apparently but I'm going to be controversial and say, no he didn't kill any dragons because there are none.

Dragons, fairies, elves, goblins, unicorns, giants, trolls and so on, have become folklore that have longevity but no substance.

The information I was investigating is different because it's verified many times over. This collection of reported incidents is consistently similar throughout the centuries. The evidence repeats itself many times over. Different generations report seeing the same things. Let me start at the beginning of the story and you can see for yourself.

IT WAS A COLD EVENING in November, and I remember pulling out a sheet of paper from the scanner and adding it to the file beside me on the polished walnut desk. More evidence of paranormal activity in the city, around the areas where the plague pits were dug and filled with the victims of the disease. People from all walks of life were buried quickly and without ceremony. Merchant shipmen lay next to beggars, their graves never marked. Is that one of the reasons there is negative energy around those areas of the city?

The article I had printed was another press clipping about a death on St Oswald's St, which was behind Brick St and joined Old Swan to Edge Lane at the junction of Rathbone Road. A priest known as Father Thomas had left a pub called The Paraffin Oil Shop, which was a place he frequented most days. Witnesses told reporters that the priest would order two double house whiskeys and take a seat at a table, placing one of the drinks opposite himself, as if someone was sitting there. He would mutter to himself, words that no one could understand. Regulars from the pub said he would toast his invisible companion and then drink the contents of both glasses. Sometimes he would repeat the process for hours, leaving blind drunk, but on the day in question, he had only had two doubles. When he left the pub that day, he had 'fallen' under a black cab and was stuck underneath it for an hour as the firemen tried to lift it off him without killing him. The black cabs of the day weighed over a ton and hydraulic jacks were brought to the scene by the fire brigade.

Apparently, the priest screamed in agony, cursing God and the Devil, speaking in a language no one understood. It was put down to the ramblings of a critically-injured man in agonising pain. Having studied the case, I have to disagree. I think he was speaking in a satanic tongue until he could scream no more. Father Thomas didn't make it and I hope he's burning in hell.

Following the removal of the vehicle and the body, the police questioned witnesses and two members of the public made statements that they had seen a young blonde girl push the priest from the pavement, but other onlookers denied that they had seen a young girl at the scene. No one else could confirm their version of events but the fact that they were saying the priest was pushed made it a murder investigation.

The police interviewed all the witnesses again and made several appeals for information but no one else had seen the girl. The two witnesses who saw her were questioned at length by senior detectives, to make sure what they were saying had credibility. When they were pressed about where the young girl went after she pushed Father Thomas under the taxi, they couldn't answer the question. One of the witnesses said she was dressed in a dark blue pinafore with white lace frills at the wrist, but he couldn't say where she went to. One minute she was there, the next, she was gone.

Most of the other witnesses said he appeared to stumble into the road and there was nobody near him, which led to the question of how much he had drunk that day. The police wanted the case closed as quickly as possible and the theory of a little girl pushing a priest under a cab was dismissed. The absence of proof that a young girl was actually there, meant the death was filed as an accident and the case was closed for a while but it refused to go away.

The 'accident' would have been talked about for a while and then forgotten but for the allegations that emerged following the death of Father Thomas. Rumours began to spread through the neighbourhood, like whispers on the wind. It was said the priest had been to see a troubled woman, who was known locally as the 'witch' because she threatened her neighbours and passers-by with curses and spells. It was clear she had mental health issues. Strange chanting and incantations were often heard coming from her house. Pets in the locality had a habit of going missing and never returning and fingers were always pointed at her.

She lived at 44 Brick Street, the scene of the brutal murder of an estate agent during Covid in 2021.

There were many rumours circulating, gaining strength and credibility; each new accusation created ripples of anger across the community. A few weeks after Father Thomas died, one woman came forward. A single accusation of long-term abuse was made and investigated and it brought with it a wave of revulsion. It was printed in the local small press and then the story was run in the Liverpool Echo and the floodgates opened.

A woman in her forties was the first to come forward. She claimed she was eight years old when Father Thomas had taken her into the vestry and raped her following her Holy Communion while her mother helped other parishioners to tidy up the church. He had told her she was special, and God wanted her to feel his love through Father Thomas. She was assaulted a further four times in the months following her communion, each time in the church vestry while her mother tidied up, brushed and mopped the church. After each rape, Father Thomas gave her a boiled sweet and swore her to secrecy. It was between them, and God and God would show his wrath if he was angered. The abused child was terrified to speak out, frightened by the threat of offending God.

The woman, whose name will remain secret for the purposes of this book, eventually found the courage to tell her mother and father about the assaults but they didn't believe her. They were disgusted by her accusations against their local priest, a man who had buried all four of her grandparents, christened her and given her Holy Communion. Her parents called her a liar and forbade her to repeat her allegation against Father Thomas ever again. Her father took her to her room and whipped her with his leather belt for daring to disrespect the priest and the Catholic Church.

After the beating from her father and the humiliation of not being believed, she maintained her silence and suffered indescribable abuse. Father Thomas continued to rape her for six years until she was fourteen, when she fell pregnant. She claimed the baby was the result of being raped by Father Thomas, but no one took her seriously. The pregnancy brought terrible shame to the family and the poor girl was sent to an asylum at Winick, Warrington. The baby was removed at birth and following twelve months re-education in a convent, where she was avowed to keep silent, she was allowed home, and the issue was never discussed again. She kept her vow of silence until the priest fell under the taxi thirty years later. Her parents were dead and buried and there was no one to fear anymore.

Over the next ten months, dozens came forward, male and female, ages ranging from their forties to teenagers. Father

Thomas had been abusing his congregation for decades. As the investigation gathered speed, allegations of Satanic rituals became prevalent. Father Thomas hadn't been acting alone in many cases.

The Satanic element of the abuse frightened people, not just those in the area but across the world. It shook the Catholic Church to its foundations. Journalists from every corner of the planet came to Liverpool and wanted to know what the priest had done and how he had been able to get away with it for so long. Why had no one spoken out before his death?

There were many victims and the one thing they all had in common was fear. They were too frightened to speak out. Many told of sacrifices and people disappearing on the holy days of the Satanic calendar. The violence was off the scale, and they had been traumatised by the abuse and were too terrified to talk about it until their abuser was dead; even then, some would not talk about the rituals. Father Thomas had not acted alone, and the other abusers were still at large, and the victims feared retaliation.

It was uncomfortable reading for me. I had encountered Satanic cults before, one in particular, and they're dangerous people. Once they have you in their sights, they are relentless in their pursuit.

The victims were consistent in their recounting of what happened to them. The abuse followed the same pattern. Father Thomas identified his victims and targeted them individually in the vestry. Once he was sure he had them under his control, they were taken with others into the crypt where things got worse. The city was horrified that this had been allowed to happen and an enquiry was launched to recover as much information as possible.

Some of the abuse took place in the church vestry, some in the crypt beneath it, but all the victims stated that the ceremonies were conducted deeper underground. The police had asked the Church to let them search the building and especially the crypt, but they blocked access for weeks, citing that they were seeking permission from Rome. They blocked the police until a judge eventually overruled them and gave them a warrant. When they finally gained access, they found the crypt had a network of tunnels leading from it in several directions, north, south and west. The crypt had been emptied and steam cleaned professionally, and the tunnels bricked up. The brickwork was new. Asked why the tunnels were sealed, the Church claimed that the tunnels had flooded, probably by a broken sewer, and that freezing cold drafts and unwholesome odours were coming from them.

The truth is more likely that the Catholic Church had been disgraced too many times and they made sure there were no blood or semen traces to be found. Why else would anyone steam clean a crypt? Father Thomas was just another priest shielded from prosecution to protect the brand of the Catholic Church and its cancer of paedophile priests. Nothing new there; they have made it an art form.

The victim statements which I have been able to read are typical of this type of abuse. Father Thomas was a paedophile and he enlisted other paedophiles to join him under the guise of ritual Satanic ceremonies, which encourage the rape of anything and anyone that can be raped. Worshipping Satan, Baphomet or any of a host of devils and demons, involve sexual acts with whatever they choose; animal or human. Many of the victims were forced to drink communal wine, which had been spiked, and their recollections are nightmarish and dreamlike. Several of the more lucid victims told of being blindfolded and taken beyond the crypt through a tunnel to a large cellar illuminated by candles, hundreds of candles. All of them mentioned the stench of decomposition and that there were men and women wearing animal and demon masks already there waiting for them. They were pounced upon immediately and assaulted.

The abuse these people were subjected to is too distressing to be chronicled in this story, but each victim was scarred mentally and physically. Dozens disclosed that they had bite-mark scars on their bodies, usually the breasts on the females and the buttocks on the males. Bite marks that were unhuman and had barely faded over decades. Most of them mention an altar and a female high priestess, who wore a goat's head headdress. Does it sound familiar to you?

I should have walked away at that point, but I was going down the rabbit hole, searching for something to tell me they were involved. Was O9A responsible again? (Please don't Google them. You will find websites and Facebook pages that will horrify you, but they have pixels in them to see who is reading them. You will find them, but they will find you in the process. This is not a joke. Don't Google them!)

The deeper into the story I delved, the darker it became. I began to wonder if the young girl seen pushing Father Thomas under the taxi was a victim seeking revenge, but only two people saw her. Her clothing sounds old fashioned and out of place but both witnesses described the pinafore dress. What are the chances of two independent witnesses making up the same story, and describing the attacker as a young, blonde female? Then both describing a dress which doesn't belong there? Millions to one. So, was she there and if she was, who was she?

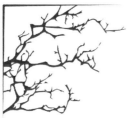

Chapter 3

I was no longer just investigating ghosts and unexplainable happenings in the Old Swan area. There was clearly a link to the Satanic murder of a man called Barry Bishop in 2021. A man is serving a whole life sentence for his murder, which involved cannibalism, but the police had tried to play it down as an isolated incident carried out by a man with serious mental health issues.

That wasn't what the evidence told me. I was staring at the existence of the long-term existence of a Satanic cult involving other paedophiles, centred around a church. It was clear from the victims' statements that there was a cult and Father Thomas had used his position of trust to feed them with victims. No one said he led the ceremonies or stood behind the altar. All the witnesses testified that the priestess was the orchestrator. A female was in charge. This is an irrefutable fact. The murder of Barry Bishop allegedly involved a female, who was never traced, but several females died in an ensuing fire when the neighbouring properties were raided. So, did the priestess die in the fire?

Father Thomas and his paedophile friends had stirred up a tsunami of anger. Accusations were being made about other parishioners and vigilante groups had attacked several homes where abusers were said to have lived. There was no evidence in the file to back this up, but mob rule is blind and angry vigilantes feed off the anger and make mistakes. But what was the connection between Father Thomas, the cult, and the unexplained incidents recorded over centuries in the area, long before they were born?

Bad things had been happening in the Old Swan area a long time before the paedophile priest was even born and it seemed that 44 Brick St was mentioned in several pieces of the compiled evidence, including a raft of press coverage of the murder in 2021. That house and the area around it were at the epicentre of all the activity. Witnesses put the priest at that house on the day he died, which could be a coincidence, but I don't like coincidences. It was more likely that the property was the eye of the storm, but why?

The church was where Father Thomas had identified his victims and I felt that it was the best place to start looking for the connections between the cult and the wider incidents. I wanted to know where the tunnels led from the crypt, and I wanted to find the cellar where the rituals had taken place. They were key for me. I was amazed the police hadn't insisted on breaking down the newly-laid bricks and searched the tunnels, but something stopped them. Something or someone. Professional curiosity alone made me want to see where they went to, so why didn't the police pursue it?

I have my own opinions on that but who am I to question how the police run an investigation? I'm no one. The Merseyside force is one of the most respected in the country and they were busy. Very busy. Historical crimes committed by a dead man were not top of the list. Anyway, I had been in the same situation before and making a noise about a police investigation will get you nowhere. But you have to remember that not all police officers are straight, no matter what rank they are. I have encountered several senior officers who were actually O9A. And several politicians and a couple of judges too, and they were pissed off that I put the spotlight on their insidious club, but fuck them and their brethren. O9A have some powerful sympathisers and power buys influence. Maybe someone with authority wanted the search hampered and put to bed, brushed under the carpet to protect themselves. Maybe.

As I studied the evidence, it was easy to become distracted. The history of the area was fascinating, but I can't go and see the past to verify the facts. I needed to see the here and now of what happened and how it all connected. Father Thomas was the most recent tangible person in the web of evil and his death was the catalyst to the disclosure of abuse. The abuse itself was part of multiple ceremonies, and the ceremonies were performed to generate evil energy. They added fuel to the flames. The pain and suffering fed their blood lust. It makes them feel more powerful and that is what it is all about. Power.

I wanted to see where it had happened for my own benefit. Finding the cellar (temple/altar) where the sacrifices and abuse took place, was paramount. It was my starting point. I had to get beneath that church.

With that in mind, I had asked the Church, via email, if I could have access to the crypt and tunnels from a research point of view but didn't even get a reply. I made some calls but the people I spoke to passed me over to someone else and hung up if I pushed the issue too hard. Eventually, they bummed me off completely. It was frustrating to say the least but hardly surprising. The police had struggled to get a search warrant, so how was I supposed to get in? I went to the top, but the number listed for the deacon of the diocese and his manager was out of order, so I decided to go to the actual church itself to speak to the current priest, whoever that might be. The website hadn't been updated for nine months, which didn't bode well.

It was twenty minutes in a black cab from town, where I was staying, and the closer we got the more apprehensive I felt. Like a moth to a flame, I knew it was dangerous but couldn't resist. The cab driver was a chatterbox and was familiar with Anglesey. He'd had a caravan in Benllech for years and was also an avid reader. He mentioned the Anglesey Murders series and his head fell off when I told him I was the author. That sparked a long conversation about the books and the places in them. He refused to take any money for the journey and insisted on giving me his mobile number in case I needed a taxi again. He was a nice man and brightened my mood no end.

When I arrived, I realised I wasn't going to gain access to the church anytime soon. The graveyard was overgrown, the grasses waist high and a thick metal chain secured the wooden gates which led into the grounds. I looked around to see if there was an easy point of access and walked the length of the dark sandstone wall which surrounded the church. The steeple was tall with a slated roof, bell tower, and brass clock. I glanced up at the face, which was turning green with corrosion. The hands were stuck at four minutes past four. (Another coincidence?) That didn't go unnoticed and the alarm bells in my mind were ringing. They were loud and persistent, but I chose to ignore them.

'Turn back.' I heard a voice say. A female voice. I turned around but there was no one there. A man walked past me, wearing a Boss tracksuit, staring at his phone. His staffie cocked his leg and sprayed on a lamppost. A lump was stuck in my throat, and I couldn't swallow. I tried to convince myself that I hadn't heard a voice, but I had. I had heard a voice warning me to turn back, a female voice. I had no doubt about it but there was no one there. Half of me wanted to leave that place but the other half questioned, why should I? What is in that church that you don't want me to find?

A double-decker bus roared by and splashed rainwater onto the pavement like a dirty great wave arcing towards the church wall. I stepped backwards to avoid being soaked and looked after the bus. A young blonde girl waved at me from the back window. She had the strangest eyes and was wearing a blue pinafore dress. My blood ran cold.

My instinct was to flag down another cab and go back to the safety of the bookshop in Lord Street, but my curiosity was driving the adrenalin through my veins. I had to know what had happened years ago, what was happening now and what was going to happen. A car horn blared and brought me back to the present. I felt like I had zoned out for a while. The traffic thundered past as people went about their business, and the world kept spinning. No one cared about the church, its history, its horrors, or why I was there. There was no need to proceed any further unless you cared about what happened. I cared.

I needed to get inside that building. I had no choice but to find a section of the wall where the huge stones were loose and uneven. Grabbing the top of the wall, I used the stones as a foothold and pulled myself up. I dropped down on the other side into the long grass with a thump. The graveyard was huge and uncared for. I had landed on top of a grave and was staring at the headstone belonging to the Evans family. I read the engraving. The last internment was David Evans, husband of Sarah Evans, buried in 2012. Those names won't mean anything to you but if I told you that David and Sarah were the parents of the first of Father Thomas' victims to come forward, the coincidence is fucking cosmic.

I was dumbstruck. What were the chances of that? There were faded plastic flowers in an urn which had lost its shine decades ago. Moss was growing on the stone, darker near the soil, lighter at the top. Woodworms scurried around the base of the headstone and a huge earwig crawled out of a small hole in the cement fixing. Its legs moved in unison, rippling from one of end of its body to the other and it fascinated me for the moment.

I stepped off the grave, feeling a sense of discomfort at standing on it in the first place. The couple buried in that grave must have carried crushing guilt with them into that hole in the ground. Their lives ruined just as much as their abused daughter by Father Thomas. Graveyards are bizarre places to be at the best of times but this one felt unwholesome and hostile. I wasn't welcome.

The wind picked up and the chill air touched my skin like the icy fingers of the dead that lingered there. The sound of vehicles beyond the wall drifted to me. Tyres splashing in the rain sounded like whispers of warning. I shivered but it wasn't against the cold. My hands were aching, the joints flaring in anger at being exposed to the wind. Arthritis had been creeping through my joints for years, some days are worse than others but the cold on my hands causes deep pains from my wrists to my fingertips. They felt like they had been dipped in ice, but it wasn't cold enough to cause that much pain. Something else was chilling my blood from the inside. Everything good in my soul was screaming at me to leave.

'Turn back...'

I shut out the whispering splashing sounds and told myself my imagination was playing tricks on me and headed towards the church entrance. As I turned the corner, I could see that it was sealed. The granite archway had a metal plate welded over it from the step at the bottom to the keystone which held up the arch. I tried to look beyond the plate but couldn't even see the door behind it. There were no cracks around the edges to peer through. It was securely shut and bolted into the stone. The church was closed, permanently by the look of it. Again, I could have walked away but the need to get inside was powerful.

I took out my phone and went back to the beginning and searched for the name of the last priest to be registered there. It took me a while, but I found her, Mildred Anderson, and I found out where she was, but it wasn't much help.

Plot 157 in that very graveyard.

She was dead. Or so it said on the Church diocese website. That was the end of the line for anyone who wasn't absolutely determined to see inside the church, but I was. I wasn't giving up. The obvious attempts to throw people off the scent were making me more determined to see what they were hiding. Someone important was throwing up roadblocks, determined to stop anyone from investigating what Father Thomas had done inside that building and who he had done it with.

So, Mildred Anderson was dead and buried in the graveyard, was she? I decided to check for myself, not knowing why I was exploring this particular rabbit hole but unable to shut my face, walk away and mind my own business.

A cold breeze picked up and blew through the long grass, making a whispering sound, like another warning from the dead. A shiver ran down my spine. Something was telling me to walk away.

Stay away.

Far away.

My instincts were telling me not to take anything at face value; don't believe anything until you see it for yourself. The Church lies. The Church is a lie. If they have lied, abused, stolen for centuries, why would I believe anything they say right now?

There was more to this than I had seen already, and my senses were telling me to follow my gut feeling. I Googled a plot map for the graveyard and headed for plot 157, which wasn't marked on the map; it only went up to 144. It could have been a mistake, but I doubted it.

I walked to the end of the graveyard and Plot 144 was the grave closest to the wall. Beyond the wall was St Oswald's Street, which meant that the other end of the graveyard was Brick Street. They were two of the main arterial roads through Old Swan. There was no plot 157, or if there was, it would be underneath the middle of the road. Was this a mistake or a deliberate attempt to stop people talking to Mildred Anderson, the last registered priest, by saying she was dead and buried?

Plot 144 was marked with a wooden cross which had been turned upside down. An inverted crucifix, the mark of the

Devil; could this get any weirder? I checked the name of the deceased buried there. Guess who?

If you guessed, Father Thomas, you would be correct. If I needed anymore red flags, this was a huge one. Why not walk away? What do you think you are going to find?

I didn't know that answer. It was as if I was cruising on autopilot, knowing I was going to crash but not changing course. I looked back at the church and guessed it was about two hundred yards to the centre of where the altar would be. The stained-glass windows were dull and cracked in places. They would have been vivid and striking in their day. Now they were dull and brooding. Looking at the building as I approached, I guessed the tunnels which had led north and west from the crypt could be beneath the path above ground, which led to the road, and then go beneath St Oswald's Street and Brick Street.

The ceremonies could have been held in a cellar beneath those streets. That was a significant find. Father Thomas and his cult of sick fuckers could have been taking their victims to a site beneath one of the most haunted streets in the country. I needed to break into the church, but it was growing dark, and I had no tools and no weapons. I needed to go back to the bookshop for the night. A movement caught my eye from the trees to my left. Two young girls with blonde hair were standing in the deepening shadows. One of them was the girl on the bus. They were holding hands, and one held a teddy bear in her other hand. It dangled as if its neck was broken. Both were wearing blue pinafore dresses. One of them waved and then they turned and disappeared into the shadows. I've never felt such ice-cold fear in my life. I felt sick to the core but couldn't stop my hand from waving back at them. That's one of the strangest things I've ever done but instinct took over. If someone smiles, you smile back. If someone waves, you wave back, don't you?

I stared at the spot where the girls had been standing for what felt like an age. The light was fading fast, and fear was making me feel cold and jittery. I walked toward the rear of the church and looked for an easy access point. The windows were too high to break in through without a ladder and carrying a ladder into a graveyard would get me arrested. The walls were thick, like a fortress, and there were no vents or grates leading directly beneath the church into the crypt. I was beginning to think it was impossible until I spotted a narrow set of steps which led down to a small wooden door. It was a leper door, fitted hundreds of years ago to allow unfortunates with leprosy to attend mass. It was made from oak and studded with metal pegs, arched at the top. That would be my way in. I took one more look around the building and headed for the road. I climbed the wall and jumped down on the other side. The relief to be away from the church was indescribable.

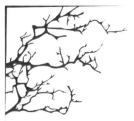

Chapter 4

It was dark when I got back to the shop. I tried to warm my hands up but struggled; my bones ached, and my head was spinning. My head was telling me to pack my bag and go home and leave the sickos to their own devices and write my stories in the safety and peace of my own house, far away from ghosts and ghouls, paedophiles and priests. The question that was echoing around my head was, would they leave me alone? I had been drawn to this place for a reason and the reason was clear. It was a trap but who was behind it?

It was obvious that the Church were desperately trying to stop anyone digging into the events of the past. They wanted the horrific events brushed into a box and the lid sealed and never opened again. I was picking at a scab and uncovering a vile truth that they didn't want uncovered at any costs. But there was more than the reputation of the Church in play here. There was something even more powerful than men and their schemes at large. There was something dark and ancient and evil looming over me. I had felt uncomfortable in that graveyard; I could feel the evil in that place, almost smothering me. It was a house of God, hijacked by something else. Something insidious. It was death, desolation, decay and despondency, so concentrated that it was tangible. You could feel it in the air you breathe and taste it on your tongue.

I made a coffee and tried to settle my nerves. I printed off the cemetery map and a tiny piece that I had found in the local online churchgoer group on Facebook. There had been no guests allowed at the priest's funeral. It was certainly food for thought as I put the article with the other evidence. Father Thomas was buried right there in Old Swan, what an insult to the community that was? He should have been burned and his ashes tossed down a toilet to float with the rest of the turds forever.

Wherever I looked there were questions. Someone had turned the crucifix on his grave upside down. Who had done that? A lover of what he had done or a hater? Was it done as a favour to his Satanic soul or as an insult, to mark what he was in life?

As I added the papers to the file, a blinding flash of light arced across the sky, forking before it hit the Earth somewhere in the near distance. A boom of thunder echoed a second later, making the windows vibrate. The storm was coming closer in more ways than one.

I was tired and poured myself a drink. I lifted a cut-glass tumbler to my lips, enjoying the aroma of a Scottish single malt. It was from the Isle of Skye and distilled into oak barrels, which were draped with seaweed and drenched regularly with spring water to infuse the whisky with the flavour of the sea. It had an almost metallic flavour, medicinal and warming. Sometimes, I could almost smell the salt air as I savoured the flavour, listening to the squawking of seagulls gliding on the sea breeze above the island's distillery hundreds of miles north but that was usually after one too many. The whisky burned pleasantly as I swallowed it. Its soothing effect settled my nerves and numbed the pain in my hands. I sat down and closed my eyes and tried to focus on one thing at a time. I wanted it to be daytime, so I could go back to the church in daylight. There was no way I could go there in the darkness of night. I don't like the dark at the best of times. I was scared of the dark as a child and I'm still not a big fan.

I had so many questions and not enough answers, but the quest was on. I read some more of the journals written by the monk, Ganzalo, and it was clear that he was shocked by what he had seen on the streets of the city during the plague. He had come to England on a pilgrimage to help the poor and sick, but he could never have anticipated the level of crisis he experienced. If his writings were to be taken as factual, not fictional and I had no reason to think otherwise, the possible answers were beginning to appear. The possible answers were stacking up and red flags were flying like a parade in China.

The curious events in the Old Swan area could be explained in different ways. They had to be different as there could be no single explanation. Paranormal investigators had written their theories for decades and many of them mentioned the monk and his journals.

When the plague came to Liverpool, it hit the city hard. It was the biggest port in the world, and all ships carried rats aboard. Obviously, rats carry disease and the living conditions at the time meant disease spread from home to home quickly. Thousands were dying daily and there was nothing anyone could do to treat the infected. It was simply a case of letting it rip through the population and see who was left standing. Thousands moved away from the cities and tried to live off the land in the more remote areas, but the inhabitants there were not so welcoming, and many were slaughtered. There are no accurate records of how many died while migrating from the more inhabited regions. No one will ever know.

There was no way that the city elders could cope with the rising death toll, so they had to implement ways to remove the diseased bodies from the streets. Men were hired and carts of all shapes and sizes were commandeered to carry the dead. Some of the men they hired were of dubious character. The opportunity to make money was obvious, even at the risk of contracting the plague. Plague pits were built at the edge of residential areas to dispose of diseased corpses. The churchyards couldn't cope with the deluge of death. No one could have seen such carnage coming and planned for it.

The gravediggers were decimated by the disease as much as the rest of society. The gravediggers left alive couldn't dig fast enough, and they were drafted to dig huge open plague pits around the outskirts of the city. One of the pits was documented as being roughly on the junction of St Oswald's Street and Edge Lane, stretching along Rathbone Road. I used to frequent a skateboard park on Rathbone Road as a schoolboy. It was popular because it had a series of ramps called the caterpillar, which was almost impossible to master. I got the last ramp once and fell off and broke my nose. (That ruined my hopes of being a model. Joke.) The designer of the caterpillar had clearly never been on a skateboard in his life. My mother hated taking me there. She didn't like the place and worried about me all day. Maybe her mother's instincts sensed the badness beneath the ground. Many of the documented ghostly sightings are linked to that part of the city. Unsettled spirits, maybe?

Why would a plague pit cause unsettled spirits to linger where they were interned, I hear you asking?

The monk's writings offer one solution to the question and it's simple.

Many of the people tossed into the pits weren't dead.

They weren't ready to pass over because they were alive. When they were tossed into the pits with the rotting corpses of plague victims, they were breathing. They may have been sick and dying, but many were not quite dead. Journals from the time quote that anyone found suffering from the symptoms, who could not walk, or talk, was put out of their misery with a blow to the back of the neck. That was not the official line but it's well documented. Some of the body carriers were religious and killing another human with their hands was a cardinal sin. Tossing them into a hole where they would die of their illness was not, so in they went.

There are many recordings of the body carriers robbing the dead and dying, rifling their houses for valuables. No one would dare search the carts that carried the plague victims and some of them became rich. Accusations of perfectly healthy people being clubbed to death and robbed before being slung into the pits, were rife. The city was in anarchy; lawless and despondent and innocent people died at the hands of criminals exploiting the situation.

So, I can accept that there are some deeply pissed-off spirits around the edge of the city. Like the birds in Southport avoiding the site of a slaughterhouse, can others sense the darkness and rather than being repulsed by it, be attracted to it? Does that darkness attract more darkness to it like a magnet? Evil absorbing evil and growing stronger.

In 1973, work began on a new school and contractors were excavating a plot of land near St Oswald's Street. The diggers moved in and uncovered an unmarked coffin at about 15ft deep. As the digging continued, more and more coffins were found. In the space of forty square metres, 3561 coffins were found, buried in a perfect square. Some of you will say that I have made that up. Google it or follow this link.

(https://www.discover-liverpool.com/local-history-stories-to-read/the-mass-graves-of-old-swan/)

They had been buried 16 coffins deep, which would indicate that they were buried in one operation. Some of the bodies were exposed and they all had holes in their skull. Were they executed and shot in the head, the evidence of a huge massacre buried in an unmarked mass grave? We don't know because all the records were lost. How convenient is that?

3561 dead people buried in a pit together with no records of who they were or why they died. Could this be another reason for unsettled spirits?

I can consider that as a legitimate theory alongside many other possible explanations. The darkness feeds off the pain and suffering of the living and there are people out there more than willing to cause pain and suffering to feed evil, so that it grows and becomes more powerful in its efforts to become all powerful and snuff out the light completely.

Father Thomas was a religious man but it's clear he was batting for the other side. The evil side. He used his position to prey not pray. He swapped God for the Devil because there were no boundaries and no celibacy. He could rape and abuse until he died. Did he find the Devil or did the Devil find him?

One thing was becoming obvious, my visit to the city where I went to school was no chance opportunity. I had been suckered in like a rat into a trap. The haunting was the bait, and I took it. Father Thomas was a Niner. I knew it in my soul. He was one of them and Fabienne Wilder, their leader, would have known him. Absolutely no doubt about it. She would have revelled in the sick fuck's achievements, rewarded him even. The atmosphere I sensed in the graveyard was evil and oppressive and now I knew why. The Niners were back on my trail with a vengeance. I had spent years hiding, running and avoiding them but now they knew where I was.

I had let my guard down. How they found me was simple. They contacted me, befriended me and then reeled me in like a fish. I had tried to avoid them for years, never revealing which part of the country I was living in, some people thought I was on Anglesey, others thought I was in Warrington, while others thought I was abroad. The truth is that I was in all of them but only my closest circle knew the truth of where and when. Moving each time they found me was exhausting and I didn't want to run anymore but they were relentless in their pursuit.

Over the years, they had sent both men and women to lure me out and most of them failed to find me. Some of them did though and two of them are in the sea, and two more are burned and buried in places they will never be found. Not in this lifetime anyway. If their remains are ever dug up by accident, I'll be long gone myself, dead and buried and beyond caring. Luckily, most of them were people who had become so wrapped up in the Niners' dark magik, they had dropped off society's radar years ago. They must cut themselves off from their families, friends, society, or 'the mundane' as they call us, when they join the insidious cult. That's part of the deal but it means if they vanish, they won't be missed. No one is looking for them, especially not the police.

The more obvious it became that this was a trap, the more foolish I felt. Foolish and scared. They knew where I was but what was their plan? It wasn't something I had time to contemplate. I had walked into their lair with my eyes wide shut. The hideous events surrounding Father Thomas were a smokescreen to blur the lines and camouflage them, so that I didn't suspect anything amiss until it was too late. I just didn't suspect their involvement.

Fabienne Wilder, their priestess, a shape-shifting demon with powers beyond my comprehension, had either changed her appearance or sent another in her place. Her new name was Galia for now. She was the same black angel, and she must have been born in the darkest pit of hell. I had never been in the presence of such a malevolent soul. She was naturally beautiful, huge hypnotising eyes, long dark hair and a disarming smile but underneath, evil oozed from every pore, belying the desolation she brought with her. Her approach was innocent and subtle.

At first, there were a few likes on Facebook posts, then some nice comments and chatting with other readers. After a few months, bedding in her fake profile, she messaged me directly and began chatting about writing, claiming she was an editor and proofreader with a master's degree in creative writing. I was invited to present at the Anglesey Writing Festival and there she was. Galia introduced herself next to the coffee machine and chatted excitedly about the festival and her disguise was complete. I never suspected anything amiss. She attended my session that day and sat through it, engaging with me and the other readers and writers in the room. I left the festival with her business card and added her to the list of freelancers I use to edit novels for myself and other authors. There was something about her, but my alarm bells weren't ringing. I certainly didn't suspect her of being an acolyte to Fabienne and it didn't cross my mind that she was actually hunting me. She had drawn me in completely.

The next step was to lure me into a trap. Galia messaged me and told me about some research she was involved in with a university group from Liverpool. They were investigating documented hauntings in the city, of which there are thousands. Rodney Street has several well- documented spooks and the cemetery at the Anglican cathedral is another ghostly hotspot. There are an estimated 58,000 bodies buried in St. James' Cemetery, and over a dozen reported spirits that haunt it. Among the various ghosts who dwell within St. James' Cemetery is the spirit of a former member of parliament, William Huskisson.

On the 15th of September 1830, Huskisson earned the dubious distinction of becoming the first person to be run over by George Stephenson's locomotive engine Rocket; that's a claim to fame if ever there was one. Huskisson's mangled corpse was entombed at St. James' Cemetery and sightings of his ghost began shortly after. William Huskisson's spirit has been seen hobbling throughout the graveyard and loitering outside his stone mausoleum, still showing the scars of being hit by train.

All the stories she sent to me fascinated me and I was keen to hear more and visit some sites. She set up a visit for me to an abandoned Victorian hospital, which I went to alone and spent an afternoon wandering the empty corridors and abandoned wards. Newsham Park Hospital is now nothing more than a shell. It has a disturbing history. Built in 1875 it was initially used as an orphanage before becoming a hospital. It spent its later years as a mental asylum before closing its doors in 1997. Sightings of ghosts are many and varied and can be traced back decades.

A nurse at the hospital became the first to complain about paranormal activity. She complained many times and wasn't taken seriously. She was found dead on a ward under strange circumstances and reported incidents increased tenfold. She was clearly an unsettled spirit, pissed off that no one listened to her. Patients reported seeing children standing at the bottom of their beds or holding hands, skipping down the corridors. The building has a strange atmosphere to it, and I enjoyed the visit. It was another ploy to bring my guard down. I talked to Galia on the phone for hours about the visit and never detected anything amiss. I was obviously drawn into the conversation and excited by the topic. She then focused on an area of the city called Old Swan and gave me a brief rundown on the history. It was fascinating. Then she told me about a curious bookshop in the city centre, where an occult librarian had made a collection of books of the occult which was unlike any other. It had become famous in those circles. The bookshop had rented accommodation for literary tourists in a basement flat beneath it. It could be rented by interested parties, who wanted to see the collection. She had only mentioned it in passing but as soon as the conversation ended, I was Googling the bookshop and planning a trip to visit it and stay in the city. The bait had been laid and the trap set, and I was oblivious.

It had always been a cat and mouse situation, sometimes I was the cat but not this time. There had been some epic battles over the years, and I had the scars to prove them. I had survived each attack, but I've always been aware that one of them would end me eventually if I wasn't careful. I survived with twelve stitches the last time, each one a reminder of this cult and their hate of me and my books about them. Fuck them.

The legacy of evil that those who take the left-hand path leave behind is sordid and vile. They are paedophiles looking for a reason to make it okay. It's never okay. They ruin lives. They're an infection in the civilised world, a disease to which there is no cure. Ending them completely is the only solution, one at a time if need be. If they could be identified, they could be hurt. They're just people. They bleed and choke and die just like the rest of us.

Unless I got back into that church, I couldn't take this episode any further though, despite its unsatisfactory conclusion. If I didn't explore what was down there, it was gone, ended, complete, finished, done. I could not walk away and feel no satisfaction or relief in its closure. I went back to the files about number 44 Brick Street and found some information which sent shivers down my spine.

There were similar unexplained events linked to an address in Penny Lane, which blew my mind. A Google search brought up a website called, haunted rooms. (hauntedrooms.co.uk) Sitting at number 4 on their list of Liverpool's most haunted places is 44 Penny Lane.

Number 4 on the list.

44 Penny Lane

My book, 44 Brick Street.

Here's another fact that you don't know. I went to school at Liverpool College on Queen's Drive and the rugby pitches and changing block back onto Penny Lane. I was a boarder there for a while and in our free time, we used to walk down Penny Lane to the shops on Allerton Road to spend our pocket money. There's another great coincidence for you. The ghost at number 44 Penny Lane is a young girl with blonde hair and she's reported to be a malevolent spirit. This information is not fiction. This is the absolute truth, and it spooks me the fuck out.

The number 4 pops up again and again. Coincidences. I don't like them.

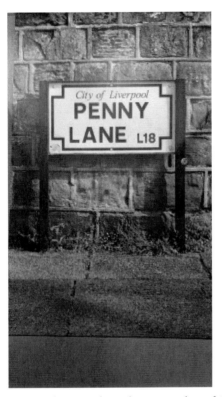

I carried on reading the research and facts behind the tragic events in that small, insignificant terraced house in Liverpool. 44 Brick Street was a brick-built residence with a history of hauntings, murders and unexplained events going back to its first occupiers. The strange occurrences had been investigated by the police, the local priests and paranormal investigators. No one could explain them. The house was a conundrum with an insidious past that seemed to seep through time to affect the present. When Galia brought it to my attention, I never thought of the possible connotations, but it was clear this wasn't a haunting by an unsettled spirit; this was evil, and evil has a source.

I should have known but my instincts were dulled by her persona. She was pretty and articulate and funny and mad about books, how could she possible be connected to the evil?

I let my guard down but that won't happen again. With hindsight, the incidences should have been red flags waving but once the ride started, I couldn't get off. I was sucked down the rabbit hole, enthralled by the horrible history of the area. The information I read didn't prove things one way or the other but at least there were some answers to the many questions I had. Granted, there were not enough answers, but there were some and some is better than none. The area around 44 Brick Street had a horrible history. Let me tell you more about the history.

Brick Street was infamous in the area for being haunted and many ghost-hunters had gone there, looking for evidence of the existence of the dead crossing back into our world. I began messaging some of these ghost hunters on social media, asking if they had heard anything about a Satanic cult being discovered at a church in Old Swan and my enquiries caused a flurry of visits by curious enthusiasts. They were like moths to a flame.

The unwanted interest from journalists and investigators provoked a response from someone involved with the cult and threats were made on social media. Things took a turn for the worse when an investigator lost her life during her visit to the area. The death was a shock to everyone. She was found dead in the small back yard at number 44 Brick Street. She should not have been there, but she had climbed a wall at the rear of the house, probably to look inside the windows. There was no clear damage or injury to her body and the ambulance crew who attended put her death down to a single critical failure such as a heart attack or aneurism. An account taken by a journalist interviewing the woman who found her body said:

'Her eyes were wide open in shock as if she had been frightened to death.'

'Frightened to death' is a saying well used when I was growing up, but I hadn't heard it for a long time. The autopsy revealed that she had a massive cardiac arrest. If she was frightened to death, what did she see?

We will never know, and sceptics will say it was a death by natural causes, but I had to put it down to the possibility that she came face to face with the evil at 44 Brick St.

She had gone there because I had made enquiries, which piqued her interest. I had overwhelming feelings of guilt for a while but if I allowed the guilt inside to get a grip, then it would never let go. Guilt is a normal human emotion but if you choose to step into the paranormal world, then normal rules don't apply. Practitioners and investigators know the risks. Good and evil lurk in the layers between us and the other planes, and they're both capable of disguising what they are, to their own ends.

Evil occupies a space and waits for a host to come along and carry out its will. Once evil finds its way into you, you are in its suffocating grasp for all time. The events documented at number 44 screamed that evil was at work in the area. Everyone who became involved in an investigation there knew the risks. Ghost hunting is a relatively safe exercise, but you might discover something else that isn't a ghost. Something evil. Evil humans, like the Niners. The Order of Nine Angles and worse, a splinter cult called The Order of Nine Angels.

I have written about the Niners numerous times, to my own detriment. With hindsight, I should never have shone a spotlight on them. When I write about them, I warn the readers, like you, not to Google them. They have pixels embedded in their websites, Facebook pages etc, which tell them who is looking at their sites. It's how they recruit. Don't allow curiosity to kill the cat. I always tell people who want to dabble with the darkness of the occult that you must be aware of the dangers.

'If you want to play with madness, then never be surprised by its ability to twist your mind. Evil will seek out your weaknesses and expose them. It will show you the horrors of the dark side just to feel your fear and make you believe. Once you believe that real evil exists, there is nowhere safe for you in this world or the next, for it will stalk you for all eternity. If you experience true darkness, and I mean pure evil, your heart never sees the light quite as it did before. Don't go looking for something you don't want to find, because you might find it.'

'Conrad Jones, listen to your own advice, you knobhead.'

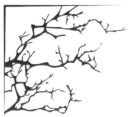

Chapter 5

That night was a long one. My dreams were haunted by the song by the Beatles, Penny Lane, and the street sign, which I had past so many times as a schoolboy. How strange it had come back into my life now.

'Penny Lane is in my ears and in my eyes...'

I couldn't get the song out of my head and images of a young blonde girl with dead eyes flooded my brain. My sleep was broken several times by phantom noises. A creaking sound, thunder, voices drifting from Lord Street. Everything was sinister and a threat. I was waiting for them to come and get me, but they didn't.

I got out of bed feeling stiff and sore and older than my years. The church flashed in my mind, and I knew today was the day that I was going to break into it and investigate the crypt. I was frightened and anxious but wasn't sure what I was frightened of. The church was boarded up and sealed. There would be nobody in there. Nobody human anyway. The ghosts couldn't hurt me, if there were any. I thought about the blonde girl and 44 Penny Lane. Was she the same girl I had seen on the bus and in the graveyard and if she was, who was she and why was she appearing to me? Or was she just a living young girl waving, and my fucked-up mindset was making up the rest?

Whatever it was, I had to go and see for myself. I ate some oats with golden syrup and gulped down a protein drink before going shopping. I bought two torches and spare batteries, a claw hammer and a wrecking bar made from hardened steel. It had a hook at one end and a chisel edge at the other. Not exactly Indiana Jones equipment but I was breaking into a derelict church, not searching for the lost ark.

I put my equipment in a rucksack, took a taxi and arrived at the church just before 11 am. The traffic was light, and it was raining; there were hardly any pedestrians about. I walked to the section of wall which I had climbed the day before and tossed the bag over first. I checked the road for any sign of police cars before climbing over and dropping onto the Evans' family grave again. I didn't linger this time. The significance of the family grave had faded. It was another coincidence in a forest of them.

The graveyard was deserted, no sign of the young girls from the day before or any other apparitions. I picked up my rucksack and walked towards the church, each step filled with anticipation. The air was cold and damp, uncomfortable and unwelcoming. I shouldn't have been there, not because it was trespassing but because it was stupid. I walked a full circuit of the church to make sure that there was no sign of an ambush. I was feeling paranoid but better to be safe than sorry. If I made my way into the church, it would be the only way out. Once inside, I would be a sitting duck coming out. It was a chance I would have to take.

I reached the steps which led down to the leper door. The stairwell was ankle deep in fallen leaves, crisps packets and McDonald's wrappers. I double-checked to see if there were any onlookers. The graveyard was empty, no sign of movement. I walked down the steps to the door and nudged it with my shoulder. It had been there since the 1700s, which should have weakened it, but it was oak, and it was solid. The handle was a heavy iron ring and the hinges looked like they would carry tons if necessary. I bent down and peered through the keyhole, but it was dark inside, too dark to see anything. The smell of decay drifted through it. The darkness in there was almost total and the shadows seemed to shift and swirl, deeper black in places. I hate the dark. *What was I thinking?*

I unzipped the rucksack and took out the hammer and wrecking bar. They felt good in my hands. I placed the hook behind one of the hinges and hammered it down between the hinge and the wood. The wood gave way and splinters flew in the air. It was old and brittle and there was an audible crack. I hammered it in as deep as I could and then put the hammer down on one of the steps. Grasping the bar with both hands, I pulled down as hard as I could. The ancient screws groaned in protest and came out a few millimetres but held. I took the hammer and struck the bar half a dozen times.

Bang

Bang

Bang

Bang.

Bang.

Bang.

Each blow wrenched the screws a few millimetres more out of the door. The noise echoed across the graveyard. I put the hammer down and wrenched the bar again; this time the screws gave way and the hinge banged against the stone wall with a clang. The sound was deafening. I froze, startled by the noise, worried someone would hear it. Getting arrested for being equipped to break and enter into a church was not top of my agenda. It would look as if I was planning on stealing things. Try explaining that one to the judge, Jones you knobhead.

I tiptoed up the steps and checked that there was no one there for the third time. No one had heard me because no one else was stupid enough to be in the graveyard of a disused church in the pissing down rain. I went back down the stairs and repeated the process with the second hinge. It gave up without too much of a fight and the wood cracked from one corner of the door to the other. I pushed it with my foot, but it wouldn't budge. I picked up the bar again and pushed the chisel end between the stone and the wood and pulled with all my might. The door split in half and clattered onto the floor. Woodlice and beetles scurried from underneath it and the rank odour of decomposition poured from the doorway. I wasn't expecting potpourri, but the stink made my eyes water. My heart sank at the thought of entering that building. The hairs on my skin were standing on end, tingling with fear. I did not want to go inside. Not that day or anytime soon.

I put the hammer into the bag and took out a torch. The bar was staying in my right hand where it could be used to deter anyone thinking of bothering me. Its weight gave me some comfort.

I switched on the torch and pointed it into the church. A narrow set of stone steps curved up into the darkness of the stairwell. I knew that leper doors were used to allow the infected to attend mass and usually led to a spot inside that was level with the altar, out of sight of the congregation. There was no doubt that the steps would take me into the church, but I hoped they hadn't been blocked.

I aimed the torch at the steps and slung the bag over my shoulder, keeping the wrecking bar slightly raised. The steps curved to the right and halfway up them, I could see the dull daylight which filtered through stained glass windows into the church. Cobwebs hung like ghostly strands, tickling my face and sticking to my skin. I brushed them away each time, making me shiver inside. I reached the top and climbed over a low rail and found myself inside the transept. The altar was raised and to my right, the nave and bell tower to my left. Everything was where it should be. A gold cross stood proudly on the altar, flanked by two golden goblets. Cobwebs hung between them, and I could see the bulbous bodies and thick legs of the huge spiders which had spun them.

Jesus was crucified to a cross, hanging from the ceiling of the apse. The effigy was fifteen feet tall at least and the detail was incredible. Jesus looked painfully skyward, tears running from his eyes. The nails in his hands and feet looked as real as any I've seen. Its cruelty was a warning to all sinners. The pews were aligned with perfect symmetry, hymn books and psalm booklets sitting in the racks next to the prayer cushions. The baptismal font was to the left of an ornate lectern, from where Father Thomas had preached to the congregation that he was abusing. What type of man can rape children at Holy Communion and preach to their parents the next Sunday? Why did he have no fear of being outed?

Everything was covered in a layer of dust but where it should be; nothing had been disturbed or put into storage. The contents of the church were complete. It was as if someone had simply decided to shut it down, locked the door, bolted a metal plate over the entrance and walked away. The air was still and calm but filled with tension, anticipation, expectancy. I could sense the building holding its breath, waiting for something. Waiting for me?

I walked down the east aisle, not wanting to annoy Jesus by walking past the altar. I'm not a fan of religion but it's best not to push my luck, just in case he is the Son of God and can still do the odd miracle. Despite treading carefully, my footsteps echoed throughout the building, bouncing off the vaulted ceilings and stone walls. I reached the belltower entrance and pushed opened the door with the bar. It creaked loudly as it swung on rusty hinges. A staircase twisted upwards, and a breeze whistled skywards, moving the strands of gossamer. To my left, another staircase twisted downwards into the crypt. It looked like an abyss.

The steps leading up were lit by the watery sunlight, the steps down were pitch black. Only a mad man would have gone down those steps without good reason. I aimed my torch into the darkness and took the first step without hesitation. If I had considered what I was doing for more than a second, I would have turned and run. I headed for the crypt.

My breathing was shallow, not from exertion but from nerves. What could be down there that was causing me such anxiety? I knew I had been tricked into coming to the city, but this could not be the site of the trap. The building had been sealed for months. No one could have survived inside, no matter how crazy they were. Even the most dedicated follower of Satan could not be lying in wait in an empty church.

I took each step down with trepidation and my determination was weakening with each step that I took. The torchlight appeared to be fading, the shadows were closing in, the beam not penetrating as far as it had. The light from above was all but snuffed out by the spiral twist in the staircase. I knew that the batteries were new, and the torch was new, so it had to be my imagination playing tricks in my mind. My brain was telling me that each step, it's going to get darker. I told myself to get a grip.

Each step I made, it did get darker, and the smell became stronger, almost choking me. The odour of human excrement was mingled with the stench of rotting meat. How could there be either of those things in the crypt?

I didn't have time to debate the possibilities. One hesitation could lead to me losing my bottle and turning around. It would all have been for nothing, and I would be none the wiser as to what they were up to. The answers might be in the crypt, and they might not but if I didn't go down there, I would never know. I kept going, one foot in front of the other, the spiral steps making me dizzy, and I was scared to lose my balance. The stone steps seemed to go on forever but eventually, I reached the bottom.

I was in the crypt. I shone the torch to my left along the foundation wall. It was dry and clean. Too clean. I remembered that the police found that it had been steam cleaned by a commercial company. They had done a good job. The floor was made from limestone slabs, worn smooth over centuries. Again, it was spotless where I could see it. There were three marble sarcophaguses at the centre of the crypt. I had no idea who was interned in them, and it didn't matter. I walked to my right using the torch to light the way. The sound of running water came to me. It sounded like it was far away. The crypt was empty but for the stone coffins.

I was disappointed, although there was relief there too. I had no idea what I thought I was going to find. The police had searched it, what could they have missed that I could find? I walked further into the crypt and noticed something on the floor next to the sarcophaguses. The torchlight illuminated a tin of Heinz beans, empty and discarded. Chicken noodle soup, beans and sausages, sardines, tuna, coke, Fanta and water bottles. They were all empty, dozens of them. The connotations ran through my mind at a million miles an hour. Who had eaten them?

I walked on and the smell of excrement became stronger. I shone the torch into the far corner and illuminated the reason strewn across the floor. Used toilet roll and hundreds of human stools. Someone had been living down there, eating cold food from tins and crapping on the floor. Was this what their plan was? Had they planted an assassin beneath the church in the blind hope that I would turn up?

Never in a million years.

This was something else, worrying, nonetheless. Where were they hiding?

I carried on towards the far end of the church and noticed some new bricks in the wall. I figured it was one of the tunnels that they had bricked up. My bearing told me it headed north. Was that the tunnel that the priest had taken his victims down?

I shone the torch along the wall and stopped in my tracks. Bricks were scattered across the floor, dozens of them, some piled up on top of each other. The tunnel heading south was no longer sealed and the bricks had been pushed into the crypt from the other side.

So, someone broke into the crypt from the other side. From inside the tunnel. Where did it go and who had used it to break into the crypt? These were the questions spinning in my mind. It looked to me like someone was hiding down there but hiding from what? The church had told the police that the tunnels were blocked off because of a burst sewer causing bad smells but they were probably lying. What if they knew where the tunnels went to and who dwelled down there?

As I headed towards the tunnel entrance, the sound of running water became louder. There was another sound, far away but clearly audible. The sound of children laughing. I knew there were two schools in the area. An infants' school and a primary school, but they were near St Oswald's church, not this one. Maybe the tunnel went in that direction and the noises were drifting from a playground. I hoped that was the case.

I reached the breach in the wall and shone the torch into the tunnel. It had been carved through the sandstone and was rectangular in shape. For those of you who know a little bit about Liverpool, you'll know that there are miles of such tunnels under the city, built by a rich tobacco merchant, Joseph Williamson. He built extensive networks of tunnels, rooms and voids and no one knows why. This tunnel was manmade, no doubt about it. It was supported here and there by brick columns. There was a slight gradient down as it led away from the church. The torchlight only penetrated so far, and the tunnel appeared to be empty. It was quiet now, the sound of children gone. Thankfully.

I ducked through the gap and started down the tunnel. The temperature dropped by five degrees at least. It was cold and damp and I didn't want to be there.

I checked my watch. 11.30 am.

I walked for ten minutes in the same direction until I found the first void. The stench was unbearable. I had to cover my nose and mouth to stop me vomiting. It explained the smell of rotting meat. The torchlight illuminated a hole about thirty feet deep and ten feet wide. It was full of animal bones in varying states of decomposition. Hundreds from what I could see. Water had seeped into the pit, and it looked like black ink. Anyone falling into that void was dead as a dodo. There was no way to climb out. Why was there a pit full of animal bones? The answer depended on who killed the animals. I could see dogs and cats, foxes, sheep, and even horses. Someone had slaughtered them and needed to dispose of the bodies where no one could see them. If the animals were stolen and sacrificed, that would fit with the fact that the Niners were still active in the area. I felt like I was getting closer to something, but I didn't know what.

I carried on and the sound of running water became louder. The tunnel appeared to be blocked ahead. I could see the white tips of foaming water. An underground stream ran from one side of the tunnel to the other. Above it, the roof had collapsed, and a huge cast-iron pipe was spilling its contents into the tunnel. The stench told me it was a sewer pipe, so the Church had been truthful about that at least, but they would never have wanted the police to go down there. There would be too many questions asked if that pit had been discovered. I wondered about whatever lay ahead. I guessed there were things down here that they didn't want to admit to.

I approached the stream with caution. The water was running fast. It was strong enough to take the legs from underneath you if you lost your footing. I put the wrecking bar into the water to see how deep it was. It was knee deep at the edge and thigh deep in the middle. If I wanted to proceed, I was going to get wet. I lowered my left leg into the freezing water and searched for a solid footing. The water pulled at my leg, trying to pull me away. I looked at the spot where the stream left the tunnel and my heart thumped. It was pouring through a hole in the wall as wide as a saloon car and it dropped steeply into blackness. One wrong step and I was going over the edge into nothingness. No one would know what happened to me and no one would care. Was this all worth it?

I shook away the doubts from my mind and crossed the stream, avoiding the waterfall of human waste pouring from the burst sewer pipe to the left. The stench was unbelievable. I climbed out and was relieved to be back on dry land but gutted that I would have to make the journey back. My feet were like blocks of ice. I stamped my feet to get as much water out of my shoes as possible and then aimed the torch down the tunnel.

The sound of laughter drifted to me. A female, probably very young. I wondered if she was blonde.

I took a deep breath and carried on. I checked my watch. 11.50 am. It felt like I had been in the tunnel for just a few minutes, but time was passing quickly down there. I set off again and walked as quickly as I dared. There were a few small offshoots, but they were only a few feet deep. Deep enough for a Niner to be hiding. I was cautious but becoming more confident as I made progress. The burst sewer main told me that I had passed under the main road; the sewers always ran along main roads. Another hundred yards and I would be approaching Brick Street.

The tunnel began to climb steadily, and the sound of the water faded. That was when I came across a pile of clothes on the floor. I prodded them with my foot. The blue jeans were a size 8, the Nike trainers were a five. A matching knickers and bra set, made from blue lace, were next to the jeans. I picked up the trainers and put my fingers inside. They were still warm.

A female had stripped off minutes before. Whatever she was doing down there, it wasn't for the benefit of good; stripping naked was like going into battle. I'm not sure but it's what they do. This wasn't going to end well. I wondered if she was watching me. Whoever she was, she was there for all the wrong reasons. A scream from my left made me freeze to the spot. I caught movement in the corner of my eye and the glint of steel in the torchlight. I raised the wrecking bar instinctively and a blade pinged loudly against it. The woman was petite and blonde, with wide dead eyes like a shark. She was screaming at the top of her voice, words I didn't understand or care to. She slashed at me again with the curved blade and again I parried the blow with the bar. Her empty hand clawed at my face, and I felt her nails ripping my cheek. She was unbelievably strong. I shoved her as hard as I could. She was thrown back off balance and slumped against the tunnel wall. I thrust the chisel end of the bar hard into her face. It pierced her left eye, popping the orb. Blood and vitreous humour splattered my face, and she squealed like a stuck pig. Her screams echoed down the tunnel. I pulled the bar from her eye and brought it down hard on top of her head. I heard her skull crack, and she stopped screaming instantly. She dropped to the floor like a marionette with the strings cut. That's when I noticed her tattoos. The woman was covered in script. Every inch of her body below her neck was inked. I like tattoos but this bitch was way ahead of me.

The tunnel became deathly silent; only the sound of the stream could be heard. I wasn't sure what would happen next, but I've seen enough horror films to know dead baddies have a habit of getting up again. I grabbed one of her tiny ankles and dragged her down the tunnel. I was puffing when I reached the gushing water but didn't rest. I rolled her into the current and watched her float towards the precipice. She went over the edge into the black void and was gone. Fuck her.

I wanted to drink from the stream but dared not risk it. Thirst was just one of my companions now. Thirst, exhaustion and fear. Was she there for me or was she some kind of guardian for whatever lay ahead?

I didn't hear the man who pushed me approaching. The force was enough to knock me off my feet. I landed face down in the stream and I floundered around trying to get a grip of something I could hold on to. I was being pushed towards the edge of the tunnel by the force of the water. My feet were slipping on the rock bed, each time I tried to stand up. I was deafened by the roaring stream and a kick to the face knocked me backwards. I felt my top lip split and tasted blood in my mouth. It took me a few minutes to steady myself and I realised that I was still holding onto the wrecking bar. I swung it towards the edge and the hook found purchase in the rock. There was a moment where I thought I was going to lose my grip and fall into the abyss. I thrashed about like a fish out of water and eventually managed to climb onto the dry land again. My breathing was laboured, and my muscles ached from the exertion. I was succumbing to the cold and the urge to curl up and lie down was overwhelming.

If I stayed still, I would die. The choice was stark but simple. I stood up straight and a blow to the back of my head stunned me. Fireworks went off in my mind. Instinctively, I swung the bar blindly and hit something squidgy. A cry of pain told me it was human. I thrust the bar at the point of the cry and felt the chisel pierce something. Another cry of pain and I heard footsteps running away and I had a respite to recover my wits about me. I tried to pick up the torch from the floor, but my fingers were frozen. I rubbed them on my clothes to warm them up and breathed into my hands.

I grabbed the torch and aimed the beam in the direction the attacker had gone. There was no sign of him, but I knew he was there somewhere, lurking in the shadows, waiting for the chance to smash my head in.

I put one foot in front of the other and headed up the tunnel. The pile of clothes was where they had been and marked my progress. I stepped over them and carried on. The tunnel was bending slightly to the left and the incline became steeper. There was no sign of the man. Up ahead about 100 meters away, I could see amber light flickering from the walls, shifting the shadows as if they were alive. My first thought was that it was candlelight. I was cold and tired and running on adrenalin as I approached the light.

I put down the torch and took the hammer from the bag. I was right about the candles, there were dozens of them. They were at the sides of the tunnel on the floor, on rock shelves carved from the sandstone, flickering and casting deep shadows. The tunnel had come to an abrupt end but widened to the right hand side. It was a cellar from what I could see but the ceiling had collapsed to expose it to the tunnel. To the left was an altar with a four-horned ram's skull at the centre. It was draped in animal skin and stained with blood. Lots of blood. I could smell its coppery odour on the air. Human skulls were being used as candle holders at each side of the ram. A huge sigil was carved into one wall, a nine-angled star at the centre. It was a big open space and could well have been where the priest brought his victims. I stepped inside and felt my skin crawl. My throat became parched, and my nostrils burned each time I drew breath. I wasn't welcome here. The air felt like acid on my skin.

I walked to the far end of the cellar, where the ceiling had collapsed and the remnants of a staircase were hanging from the wall, charred and blackened by fire. The exit was completely blocked by a collapsed building above. I wondered if it was one of the houses on Brick Street. Behind me was a collapsed wall, which led into the cellar of the next building. It was a burnt-out shell, but candles burned on every inch of floor. I climbed over the debris and walked across to the next wall. There was a rectangular door, which showed no signs of being damaged by fire. Without thinking, I twisted the handle and opened it.

The door led into a cellar, which was completely intact, and I stepped inside. There was an empty wine rack on one wall and a workbench fastened to another. A washing machine and tumble drier were fixed beneath a wooden staircase. The drier was rumbling as the drum turned. I had walked from the pit of hell into modern suburbia in just a few steps. The house above was like a portal to another world, used by the Niners even now. Some of their houses had been ruined in the fire at number 44 Brick Street but not this one. This one had survived and was cleverly hiding in plain sight, disguised as a mundane terraced house in a street where people have been 'unlucky'.

I looked around and found the water main, running beneath the stairs. Above it was the gas main. I walked up the stairs and opened the door, waiting to be attacked. It led into a small kitchen that belonged in the seventies. I was shocked to hear a woman singing to herself. She sounded like my Nanny Kelly, my Mum's mum. and the kitchen was identical. This was a head-fuck. They were playing with my mind.

I felt behind the door. The key to the lock was on the other side. I took it and closed the door, locking it from the cellar side. My next move was a gamble and if I lost, I would be roasted alive. I went back down the stairs.

I took the hammer and smashed through the gas main, hoping no sparks would be created. Pressurised gas poured through a hole the size of a cricket ball and I turned and ran. I scrambled through the cellar door, leaving it open, and navigated myself through the burning candles, past the altar and into the tunnel. The gas would fill the basements and reach the candles and when it did, anything in that tunnel and beyond was toast.

I found a second wind as I sprinted down the tunnel. The oppression was lifting. I could feel it with every step and then I realised that the woman's clothes were gone. It didn't matter; there wasn't time to dally. I crossed the stream in two leaps and was barely wet. All the time I was waiting for an explosion and a fireball to race down the tunnel and barbeque me, but I made it to the crypt safe and sound. My lungs were burning.

There was no time to rest and gloat. I crossed the crypt and bolted up the spiral staircase into the bell tower. The church felt strangely brighter than it had, as if a fog was lifting. It might have been in my mind, but it felt different. The tables had turned. I ran through the nave to the transept and jumped over the rail into the leper entrance and climbed down the steps. I was outside and in the fresh air and it had never tasted so good. I dumped the hammer and wrecking bar down the steps and made my way to where I could climb the wall.

I was getting into a taxi to get back to the city centre when the gas main exploded. The stained-glass windows blew out and orange flame billowed through them, spiralling skyward. Plumes of thick black smoke climbed from the church, dwarfing the bell tower, and I knew that they were done.

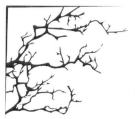

Chapter 6

Evil had focused on that area and refused to release its grip. Let me share some more of the history of Brick St in order to illuminate what I think happened. There were a catalogue of events dating back to the late 1600s. They were well documented and proved that there is a dark shadow over the area, especially where the Tesco store now stands. It took a lot of digging and talking to people who did not want to talk about their experiences, but some of the root causes can be identified. I hope that the publication of this story puts the blame fairly and squarely where it belongs. There are people to name, shame and blame and others who were innocent bystanders. People are responsible for their actions and for the actions of the dark forces they summoned but I don't know, even now, if this evidence will be believed. Despite researching it, studying it and compiling it, I find it hard to believe it myself.

The evidence led me to uncover weird tales, mysterious happenings, unexplained events and incidences of complete horror, which were masked on brief occasions by periods of happiness but in unequal measure. Happiness and tragedy, life and death. Isn't this just life?

Not in this case. Trust me when I say that the natural balance of the universe is just that. Balance being the operative word.

44 Brick St was an address tainted by murder and mayhem for most of its history but so was the area prior to the house being built and this is an important fact. The evil was already there before the house was built. The balance is heavily in favour of evil events and happy times are at a minimum.

There are stories of young newlyweds, which were sad enough to make the strong weep. One couple in the 1600s were plagued with illness soon after moving into the area and they struggled to conceive. Rumour has it this was 1644, the husband sought a fertility potion from a local witch and things went from bad to worse. The wife gave birth to four mutated children, which the local legends say were goat like in appearance, living for only minutes but howling like animals before they died. None of their bodies were buried. They were burnt.

They had another child who was described as lupine, and the midwife who delivered her was bitten by it before it too died. Her wound became infected, and her arm was amputated but not before the infection had spread. She died in agony four weeks to the day of the birth.

The witch was prosecuted, and the judge ordered that she was boarded until she confessed to being a witch and being responsible for the deformed children. She was taken to the market square, and a stable door was placed on her. Heavy weights and rocks were placed on the door, but she remained silent until just before her death when she laid a curse on the settlement and the descendants of all involved in her case. The couple were accused of being cursed, and excommunicated. They were driven from the settlement by suspicious neighbours and their home was burnt to the ground. Writings from a local monk say that the wife hanged herself four days after giving birth to quadruplets, four goat-like abominations which died within minutes of being born. The husband was rumoured to have contracted leprosy and died in a fire four months later. You may have picked up on the repetitive appearance of the number 4 again?

The journals of the monk have been carbon dated and verified to be from that time. He could have no knowledge of what would happen centuries later at number 44, could he?

This was just one instance on record. The local records indicate that generations later, relatives of the judge who sentenced the witch were tied up in their home, robbed, raped and burnt to death by four men who were arrested and executed. Have a guess how they were executed.

Hung, drawn and quartered...

Cut into 4 pieces. Coincidence.

A parchment map of the area dated from the late 1700s shows a rock named as Brunt Boggart. This was a common marking from those times and translates as Burnt Witch. The rock would be roughly where Brick St is now. There are records from another clergyman who wrote about a witch on Penny Lane, who had her neighbours terrified. He wrote that deliverymen could not get their horses to walk down the street, and milk and coal had to be carried by hand to the houses. What could the horses sense, that scared them so much? The witch travelled the area north of the city selling her spells and potions. Did the couple who couldn't conceive buy their potion from her? 44 Brick Street and 44 Penny Lane. Is that a coincidence too or is that the area she cursed? I don't think it's coincidence.

There are too many stories to argue with. Every area has its rumour and folklore, but most have a balance. As I pointed out earlier, there is no balance here. The evidence is there to make of as you will. Tales from the distant past can rarely be verified one hundred percent and hearsay is twisted and exaggerated from generation to generation but there are too many of them in this case to be a coincidence. Something was rotten in Brick Street, as if the ground and the air itself were tainted with badness, poisoned by evil. I know for sure that dimensions merge sometimes but in the dimension of ancient dark Magik, coincidence doesn't exist. (Magik is not a misspelling. It's different to what we know as magic.)

Galia had pointed me in the direction of Brick Street, knowing that I would be enthralled by the history of the place, wound me up like a clockwork toy and then let me whizz off in the right direction. I had booked into the occult bookshop and was on my fourth night when things came to a head. That night, I was feeling the weight of something that I couldn't fathom. Yes, I was tired from the events in the tunnel but there was something sapping my strength. It was time to try to sleep, although nowadays, I barely get more than a few hours before the nightmares begin.

I remember moving from the desk and I switched off the reading lamp and was immediately aware of something watching me. Something, not someone. It happens a lot and I have to shake it off. Deciding to have another whisky before bedtime, I made my way from the study to the tiny living room, where a coal fire was burning in the hearth. The embers glowed orange and seemed to pulse, as if breathing. Suddenly, the flames flickered and jumped as if being fuelled by an invisible draught. There was a shift in the room. I felt it. The fire felt it too. It cast a warm glow around the room, although the corners were still hidden in shadows, which advanced and deepened as the flames danced. They darkened and swirled, making shapes that faded and vanished. It seemed that I was in a constant battle with the shadows at the corner of any room but that night, they tried to advance and engulf me at every opportunity. Every time I turned my back, I felt the darkness creeping closer.

The darkness had taken on a different form. It was no longer just shifting shadows, it was a living, breathing entity with a life of its own and it was carrying evil incarnate. I sensed it. It's difficult to explain without sounding crazy but I knew that it was trying to frighten me, break me, but I was determined that it wasn't going to happen that night. It would win the battle one day. One day it would overwhelm the light and envelop me. It would absorb me into itself, making it a little darker and a touch more evil than it was before, adding the power of each soul it absorbed. For now, I would use every ounce of power that I had to fend it off. I am alive and have the energy to keep the evil at bay, but it won't always be that way. It can't break in unless I show weakness.

I knew that night was different. There was something orchestrating the shadows. Something powerful and malevolent. I could feel the intensity of hatred it brought with it. The fire was blazing and the curtains drawn, but the cozy feeling had gone, replaced by dread.

As I told you earlier, I was renting the basement flat beneath the bookshop. The flat was basically a library containing thousands of books relating to the occult. You may think that this was an evil place, but it was the opposite. Number 9 Bold St had become an infamous sanctuary to all who stepped into the dark world of the occult and were being targeted by evil. Some still think occultism is a joke, a place where idiots find solace with other idiots; witches and wizards and wrinkled old druids prancing about Stonehenge, but don't mock what you don't understand.

There have been far more intelligent beings on this planet than us. Ancient civilisations have been here before us, there can be no disputing that. Take a look at the thousands of structures constructed using rocks so heavy that we don't have cranes big enough to move them today. Blocks of stone cut so accurately that they couldn't possibly have been placed there by the humans of that time.

The ancient city of Baalbek is one of the greatest archaeological mysteries of all time. Located east of the Litani river in Lebanon, Baalbek is known for its monumentally scaled Roman temple ruins. These Roman temples were built on top of an even more ancient 5 million square foot platform that was made from some of the largest stones ever used in any construction project ever used. The largest stone found weighs 1200 tonnes and is about 64 feet long

Who moved those stones and cut them to shape with only axes and stone hammers? Google the ruins in Malta and read the evidence. There are underground dwellings far older than the pyramids of Egypt, with disc-shaped doors made from rock, which weigh tons, yet can be slid into place by a single person. History would have us believe that when they were built, humans were running around with spears and cutting rock wasn't even thought of. Ancient civilisations, ancient intelligence, ancient evil.

There are forces in play on this world and beyond that we don't know or understand.

I had been sent to the Bold Street address by Galia and because it was such a unique collection of books. It was the bait, and I took it. I jumped at the chance to stay there and do some research, as she knew I would, but I still didn't know what she wanted.

The front of the address was a small bookstore, specialising in out-of-print editions. It had few legitimate local customers, but it had many visitors, who were interested in the occult and travelled to the city to see the collection. Away from the eyes of the public, in the basement flat, the Librarian had accumulated a private collection of books, which lined every wall. Wicca, The Books of the Dead, The Encyclopaedias of the Damned, The Nature of the Beast, Satanism, Paganism and the Sigil of Baphomet were just a few of the listings. All the dark religions were represented within the thousands of pages of documented dark arts. I had read but a fraction of the powerful works that the Librarian had guarded, and it would take me two lifetimes to read them all.

The knowledge which they imparted could be used to help others battle the darkness, but it came at a price. Sometimes while I was there, I felt the insidious energy which was held within the pages bleeding into the atmosphere of the room. At other times it was almost claustrophobic. It was like static electricity before a thunderstorm and yet at other times I felt nothing at all. My dreams were haunted by the eyeless faces of the dead authors who had written the Magik, although I had no time to pity them. They were lost to the evil side and couldn't be saved.

My focus had to be on myself, my mental health, and living as long as possible. Saving myself was the remit. I can remember glancing up at the clock on the mantelpiece and sighing inside. Nearly midnight.

My mind was still working overtime, the details of the tunnel still jostling for attention. I didn't think I would be able to sleep, even though my eyes were sore, and my body was exhausted. As I poured myself another scotch, I heard the clock chime. It was the witching hour and cold fingers of fear toyed with my mind, sending a shiver up my spine. I knew something was about to happen. Something evil was approaching at speed. I remember a knock on the living room window nearly gave me a heart attack. I heard a key scraping into the lock. I was convinced that they had come for me.

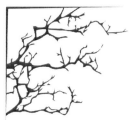

Chapter 7

I waited for the door to open, my breath trapped in my chest. The man who stepped inside smiled and took off his trilby hat. He held out his hand.

'Sorry to drop in on you like this but we need to talk,' he said. 'I'm Arthur Cross and this is my bookshop.'

My sense of relief was overwhelming. I was convinced that the Niners were there. Arthur has an uncanny aura around him, which put me at ease. We had a lot in common and the conversation began with him telling me that he had heard about an explosion beneath Brick Street.

'Was that you?' he asked, pouring himself a whiskey.

'I wanted to see what was below the church and stumbled into a tunnel,' I said. 'I followed it to a number of connected cellars, which were clearly being used by O9A.'

'Yes indeed,' he said. He took out a pipe and lit it with a lighter. 'You don't mind, do you?'

'No,' I said. 'It's your flat.'

'You have created a paradigm shift in the accusal,' Arthur said. 'Things are going to happen very quickly now.'

'I'm not going to pretend I understand what you mean,' I replied. 'What is going to happen?'

'You have heard of the book, The Abomination of Desolation?' Arthur asked, as if it was a best seller that everyone had heard of.

'I have heard of it in some of your books,' I said. 'It's more than just a book, isn't it?'

'You must have felt its effect while you've been here,' Arthur said, nodding. 'It drains your energy and sucks the life from you.'

'It has felt draining being here,' I said.

'Now you have destroyed their nest, they will flee and find another,' Arthur explained. 'But they can't leave without that book.'

'So, the book is here, in this shop?' I asked.

'Locked away,' Arthur said. 'It was safe, protected from them, but I can't protect it anymore. They will come for it tonight.'

'Oh fuck,' I said, frightened. 'I was hoping they would just fuck off and leave.'

'They can't go without the book,' Arthur said. 'You need to take it and put it somewhere they can never find it. No one must ever know where it is, not even me.'

'Why can't we just burn it?'

'It cannot be burned or torn apart,' Arthur explained. 'Take it and put it somewhere it can never be found.'

'Like where?'

'You will think of something, that's why you're here. One of them handpicked you for some reason. They know that my time with the book is over, and I have to pass it on,' he added, like I should understand. Arthur went into the back of the flat and I could hear him rummaging around in an anteroom. He came back with a wooden box, which was fastened closed with metal bindings. 'Where is your car?'

'On Brownlow Hill,' I said.

'Is it quick?'

'Very,' I said.

One thing I was certain about was that on a motorway, nothing could keep pace with that car. He handed me the box and patted me on the shoulder.

'Get going. They know it is here and they'll be here soon.'

'What about you?' I asked, heading for the door.

'I'll keep the fuckers busy for a while,' Arthur said. 'I have a few tricks up my sleeve. Don't ever come back here and don't try to contact me.'

THERE IS ENERGY IN everything on this planet and powerful elements have shaped it for millennia. Fire and water are the most powerful elements that we can fathom but we can't always control them. Both have the power to cause devastation and death to humankind. Arthur had told me that the book could not be consumed by fire, so that left only one thing.

I hit the M62 in the early hours of the morning and put my foot down. I drove for my life, knowing nothing could follow me. The motorway was quiet and when I reached the A55, the outside lane was open most of the way. I put the book somewhere it could never be found unless I told someone where it was, and even then it would almost be impossible to recover.

What if they find me and take me to find out where I put it? I won't remember soon, so I'm not overly concerned. My memory started to fade soon after I disposed of it. I have lost the ability to make new memories and am struggling to finish a sentence. Names, dates and times have gone. I sit in front of the laptop, not knowing what I'm going to write about. I'm losing my mind at a rate of knots that's unnatural. Is it a cruel disease that has been creeping up on me or is it something to do with the time I spent in the vicinity of that insidious collection of text? At this rate, in a few months, I won't know or care...

The End

Manufactured by Amazon.ca
Acheson, AB

13169419R00102